Heinemann
New Windmills

Storm

I've never told this to anyone before, at least not all of it . . .

Buck and Tunes have been friends ever since they can remember. Buck Smith is a white descendant of settlers from England; Tunes is descended from slaves brought from Africa to work on the Smiths' farm. Raised together among the creeks of Chesapeake Bay, they form a strong and loyal friendship.

But the sudden and horrifying events of a spring afternoon shatter Buck and Tunes's world . . .

About the Author

Suzanne Fisher Staples was born in 1945 and grew up in Pennsylvania. She worked as a news reporter in Asia for twelve years with United Press International. While she was in Pakistan she became involved with the nomads of the Cholistan Desert and afterwards wrote her first books, *Shabanu* and *Haveli*.

It was while she was living on Virginia's Eastern Shore in her native America, however, that she was inspired to write *Storm*:

> *There on the Chesapeake Bay, the mud and the pines and the grasses and the water and all the things that live in and among them spoke to me like characters in a book.*

Now a full-time writer, Suzanne lives in Florida with her husband and continues to pursue her love of stories and story-telling:

> *Stories are the most important thing in the world. They teach us how to live, how to love, and, most important, how to find magic wherever we are.*

STORM
SUZANNE FISHER STAPLES

Heinemann
New Windmills

Heinemann Educational Publishers
Halley Court, Jordan Hill, Oxford OX2 8EJ
A division of Reed Educational and Professional Publishing Ltd

OXFORD MELBOURNE AUCKLAND
JOHANNESBURG BLANTYRE GABORONE
IBADAN PORTSMOUTH (NH) USA CHICAGO

Text © Suzanne Fisher Staples
First published in the USA 1996 by Farrar, Straus and Giroux
First published in Great Britain 1998 by Julia MacRae,
a division of Random House
First published in the New Windmill Series 1999

03 02 01 00 99
10 9 8 7 6 5 4 3 2 1

ISBN 0 435 13048 X

Cover illustration Anne Magill
Cover design by Philip Parkhouse Design Consultancy
Typeset by ➚ Tek-Art, Croydon, Surrey
Printed and bound in the United Kingdom by Clays Ltd, St Ives plc

Acknowledgements

I am deeply grateful to the following people who shared knowledge and insights that made the writing of this book possible: to Arthur Nehrbass, whose understanding of crime, law, human nature, and writing were invaluable; to H. Mapp Walker, who knows the tides and winds of the Chesapeake Bay like they're kin; to Thadie Walker, whose knowledge of what blooms when and where is an art of itself; to Caroline and Linwood Walker for their hospitality; to Curtis and Carolyn Jones, who know and love farming; and to Betty Levin and Martha Walke, kind but unsparing readers whose knowledge of books and life kept me on track.

Chapter 1

I've never told this to anyone before, at least not all of it. All through Sheriff's investigation and the court proceedings, I only told what they wanted to know, the facts – what I saw, what I did. I never told all that happened or how I felt about it. A murder comes hard to anyone, especially a twelve-year-old, mixes him up so's it can take years to get straight again. It's been five years now and this is the first time I felt I could lay it all out, just as it happened. I'll start at what feels like a beginning.

It was early spring that year, a season of dangerous skies. I was of an age when I'd wake up before sunrise with nothing but fishing on my mind. Some mornings were so sweet and cold and clear – still a few stars, a soft thick mist rising up from the glassy water.

I could have the skiff out on the creek in nothing flat. She was a light wooden boat, and low to the water, built with all the skill and love in an Eastern Shoreman's hands. I painted her dark green every year, scraped her clean of barnacles to keep her floating like a feather. My granddaddy'd built her, and she was my proudest possession.

It seemed a sin to turn on the engine in the quiet, with the rails still sleeping in the cordgrass, and the bullfrogs and peepers and other night creatures not up yet from winter. It was about as peaceable as any place on earth.

I could be down at the bend in front of Bartons' dock just before the sun was up, slapping my fingers against my thighs to warm them. The creek meandered down there; the ghosty hulks of old skipjacks run aground showed where the shoreline had been other years. It always seemed sad those beautiful old boats would never part baywater again.

Just there the clouds would loom and menace, so cold and wet you could feel them hover. If I kept on, more like than not I'd have a right smart skiff full of icy water to push home.

It was just one such Saturday morning when it all began. Through my bedroom window the faintest tangerine glow marked where the sky met the water. Soon as I threw back my woollen blanket, old Obie's tail whumped the floor. I swear that dog loved fishing more than I did.

By the time I had shivered into my jeans and flannel shirt and down vest, Obie was stretching and making groany noises in his throat, just dying to get out on the Bay.

There was something very special and secret about being quiet in the kitchen before sunrise, with the whole rest of the house asleep above me. My feet knew every chair and table leg, every creaky floorboard; the palms of my hands knew just where each door hinge squeaked. Obie drew in his claws and puffed up the pads on his feet. Every other minute of the day that Lab clattered around like a sackful of oyster shells.

A storm had come up the night before. Branches whipped and broke in the giant cedars all round the house, and somewheres near dawn it went away, suddenly as it'd come on. Limbs littered the winter-brown lawn down to the water, and the cordgrass lay flat at the edge of the creek. Those easterly spells slammed into the mouth of the Chesapeake with ferocity and trapped the high tide in the Bay and creeks like a giant stopper.

2

Part of our dock was still underwater. The creek was calm and still, but for a fast-moving tide that sucked at the pilings. My rubber fishing boots were slick and wet to the knees by the time we got to the boathouse.

I took my fishing rod, tackle box, net and sounding pole out of the shed on the shore end of the dock. I could get in a good couple of hours hanging around the inlets up the creek, fishing for flounder or anything that'd bite. I was to meet Tunes at Bartons' dock at eleven. We were headed down to our special place on King's Creek to rake us some clams. April was early for clamming, but we always tried to get out by Easter. Night before, I'd sharpened my knife and could pretty near feel those cherry-stones slide one by one, all slick and salty, down my throat.

Tunes Smith had been my best friend ever since I could remember. We'd grown together from infancy. Her daddy, Kneebone, was manager of my father's farm, like his father and his father's father before him, all the way back to the time when they were freed from slavery, which was how they first came to work the Smith land.

Tunes' mama had worked in our house, cleaning and cooking. Once Tunes was born, just a month after me, her mama brought her along and looked after the two of us babies together. After Tunes' mama died some two years later, Gran and Mama looked after Tunes like she was their own. When Tunes and me started school, Mama had Tunes' Aunt Mazie teach her to do cornrows. She sat Tunes before her on a stool and made her recite her times tables while she braided row after row. Mama and Gran gave Tunes over to Kneebone when he came in from the fields each evening.

Mama felt sorry for her. 'Poor little motherless child,' Mama'd say, packing up nut bread she'd baked extra for them. Sometimes it'd be a slab of ham, or extra crab cakes. She'd hand me the bundle and say, 'Take it to them, son.

What can become of a girl without a mama?' But it seemed to me Tunes and Kneebone made out just fine.

Nobody knew the Bay and the fish and the tides and winds as well as Tunes. It was all pure instinct with her, like the elements dwelled in her heart, and pure bay-water pumped through her veins. She was proud of it and was sometimes right intolerant of folks who didn't know all that she did.

We were to turn thirteen that summer. It was 1991, and as I recall, even if what happened the day I'm telling you about never did happen, things were going to change right soon anyways. Fact was, Tunes would never have been able to put off facing up to being a girl any longer.

Up till then she had more respect around the fishing docks than most watermen. The watermen respected women as women, but not as fish finders, and Tunes could find fish better than any living thing on the Eastern Shore, better even than Obie, and Dad used to say he was 'bout the eighth wonder of the world.

The sports fishermen who hung out at Bartons' Fuel and Bait Dock would want to know where we'd been, what was taking bait, what kind of bait we'd used, how deep we'd fished, how fast the tide was running – everything save the length of your toenails was of interest to those sportsmen, most of them too lazy to go out and see for themselves.

Most of the sports were come-heres, retired folks moved down from up North, or folks who just came summers. They fished from big old stinkpots and wouldn't know a jimmy from a she-crab if it wore a sign.

They thought we were quaint, if somewhat backward – peculiar, with our old-fashioned language. Some Shore folks still talk like their ancestors in England. The come-heres took note of the fact we said things like 'shoal' when they said 'shallow' and that 'poor' to us was not bad but good, or that many folks still used the word 'Negro', instead of 'African American' or 'black', when that's what many of the black folks said themselves. And a fair lot of those come-heres only knew what we told them about fishing.

Any other black girl but Tunes Smith they wouldn't have expected to have much sense about anything. Tunes only ever told what she wanted, and if she and I found a really good fishing hole where the croakers were hunkered down in the green coolish bottom just waiting for us to come back in late afternoon, Tunes would tell them about a second-best place somewheres else, one maybe that even looked better than our fishing hole. It'd be better than a hole any one of them would've found.

And then, the summer before, some things happened that were irreversible. Tunes shot up in height, so that my reddish head, which used to be about even with her eyebrows, came only to her chin. I noticed her long skinny legs had started to round a little, and other places, too, so that I was embarrassed to look below her chin. Those wise, curious eyes looked different, like they could swallow you up. Instead of mischief, they looked like they held secrets. I began to wish with all my heart things would go back to where they'd been just the year before. But I knew sure as Colonel Pickett's apple trees bloomed every April things were different as they could be, and they weren't going to change back.

The questions had started to be different. Everybody was more interested in where Tunes and me had been. I mean, where had we *been*? – not where had we been fishing. We must've been a sight that spring, her tall, slim and muscular, with cornrows, and me short and poky, with freckles and skinned knees. I didn't think much about it at first, but before long all the looks and questions were getting on my nerves.

But I'm getting ahead of myself, and Lord knows it will

be hard enough to tell it straight even if I just stick to things as they happened, one by one.

As the skiff glided toward the mouth of the creek, I heard the steady pant of Doke Watkins's boat rounding the bend behind me. I'd been concentrating on looking for signs of a storm, but the soft dawn had ripened into an opal sky, and I knew we were in for a good day's fishing. I turned to see the *Dora Mae's* low, sleek hull narrow the distance to the last channel marker in the creek. The deck was piled high with bushel baskets, and Doke bent over a wooden barrel full of bait.

Doke's yellow Lab, Pup, a thin scarred male, straddled the gunwales in the prow. His tattered ears perked up when he saw Obie. They'd tangled a few months back when Obie'd made the mistake of going too near Pup's dock. Pup was a legend on the Eastern Shore. He killed water snakes and dived for skate on the creek. He never went crosscountry like other dogs'd do, following a scent. He always swam. I saw him swim by our place one day, fire-bent for someplace, and we're two mile downstream from Doke's.

Doke doused the lights in the wheelhouse then, came out and waved.

'Where ye bound, Buck?' he shouted.

'I'm going out to find me some flounder, maybe some crabs.'

'You best keep an eye out for a storm.' Doke waved and headed the *Dora Mae* north outside the creek for his crab pots. We turned south and headed for a fishing hole I'd been wanting to try.

I was setting a minnow on to my hook when I felt the boat quiver. Obie was up on the gunwales, legs bent, head a foot from the water, and that meant fish. I fished across the hole a couple of times and took in a right smart mess, including one flounder big as a doormat, then left for a while to let the hole cool down.

Most times Tunes would have come, but Kneebone had said he would set her to doing chores that morning.

I turned up Little Creek, just one down from Pungotuck Creek, where we lived, to see if I could find some blue crabs. I dipped into my bait bucket and found a dead silverside big enough to gill-string. I was criss-crossing the edge of the marsh, dangling the line over the side and not paying much attention to where the tide was carrying me, when I heard a large-sized outboard motor in toward shore.

A faint land breeze had come up, carrying shore sounds over the water. A deep voice rumbled above the chortle of the idling motor. A narrow island of salt marsh lay between me and the shore, and I couldn't see the boat at first. I looked around to get my bearings.

My heart leapt into my mouth as I realized I'd drifted into Jumbo Rawlin's territory. James Beauregard Rawlin was mean as a green-eyed snake, and he didn't hold with kids being anywhere near his property on land nor water.

The Rawlin family had been on the Shore since the 1700s, like my family. Over the years they'd bought up land wherever they could, and Jumbo had become the biggest farmer in Northampton County, Virginia. He farmed more than two thousand acres, and he stood six foot seven, every inch lean, mean, and ill intentioned.

One Sunday, Tunes and me saw Miz Rawlin out on the creek rowing like the devil was after her. Miz Rawlin was a pretty woman, younger than Jumbo, his third wife. I used to see her down at the post office in Eastville, and she'd smile and talk to me. She could do tricks, like pull a quarter out of your nose. She was tall, with long dark hair.

I pulled the skiff over to say hello. We thought it was

kind of funny she was out there without a motor. When we got close we could see her face was all swoll up, one eye bruised shut. She put her head down and waved us to go on.

Mama said she had some kind of illness and had to go away. But one thing's sure, she lit out for somewhere that Sunday morning, maybe back where she came from up North. But she never was seen again on the Eastern Shore.

Down at the docks they said of a Saturday night Jumbo'd drink a snootful of whiskey and sometimes get into fights. Another thing was Jumbo Rawlin hated dogs, and was known to kill them if they came on his property. But on the Shore many respectable gentlemen were known to tip a cup. And loose dogs killed deer and chickens, and generally raised a ruckus, so nobody looked sidewise at a farmer who shot dogs that ran.

While he was pleasant enough to grownups, Jumbo growled at kids when nobody else was around to hear, and we weren't at all sure he wouldn't do to us what he did to wandering dogs. To Tunes and me, he was bigger and badder than real life.

One time the fall before, Tunes and me were fishing on Little Creek upstream of Jumbo's place. Jumbo came along in his eighteen-foot runabout. We thought he was going to holler at us for being around his property. But he never said a word. Instead, he reached down and came up with his .22 rifle. He lifted it slowly and looked down the barrel, through the sights, straight at us.

'Wait!' I shouted. 'Don't shoot!' A place right between my shoulder blades began twitching wildly. I was so scared I couldn't breathe right, like someone'd punched me in the solar plexus.

With that, Jumbo squeezed the trigger and a little splash went up just eight inches or so behind the skiff. Tunes clamped a hand on either gunwale. Her mouth was frozen open like she'd've screamed if she hadn't been so scared. Tears ran down her cheeks, but she wasn't really crying.

'Hey!' I shouted, my voice cracking with fear. 'Stop it!' Jumbo pulled the trigger again and again and again, each time missing us by six inches or so, stopping calm and deliberate as you like to reload the gun. I pulled the starter rope on the skiff motor, but my hands were shaking so hard I couldn't pull it straight. It took several times, and it seemed half a lifetime before the motor caught and we got on out of there.

Jumbo couldn't follow us because of the shoal bottom, and soon as I realized we were clear of him – he was nowhere to be seen – I laughed out of sheer nervous energy and bravado. Tears streamed down my face, too, and my hands shook worse than ever.

But Tunes would have none of my mood. First thing she did was lean out over the side of the skiff and be sick. She put her hands into the cold, brackish water and splashed it over her face, closed her mouth, and spat it back out.

Then she turned back toward where I sat in the stern with the most dead-serious expression I'd ever seen on her face.

'He'd'a soon as killed us, Buck,' Tunes said. Her voice was shaky and low. I stopped laughing. Something about the way she spoke made me believe her. 'Promise you won't tell anybody what happened.'

'But . . .'

'We're not supposed to be anywheres near his property. And who do you think will believe us? Promise!' It was with misgivings that I promised, but I did.

What Tunes'd said was true. Dad and Kneebone'd both warned us many a time to steer clear of the Rawlin property. It was marked with NO TRESPASSING signs every few feet along the waterway and road, so there was no question of mistaking it.

As for whether anyone would have believed Tunes and me if we'd told Jumbo had shot at us, folks didn't tend to think badly of Jumbo Rawlin, and they might not have taken us seriously.

Tunes never mentioned that incident again, and so I tried my best to forget about it. But it put the fear of the Devil in me where Jumbo Rawlin was concerned.

Some years before, when farmers were having a rough go of it, Jumbo sold off a large parcel of land to real estate developers. He used the money to buy up land other poor farmers had to sell to pay their taxes. I remember my granddaddy calling him a bloodsucker, but Dad always said anybody who gave as much as Jumbo did to the church must be God-fearing. You couldn't blame a man for making money: it wasn't his fault folks'd fallen on hard times.

Jumbo Rawlin was a pillar of the community, folks said, because he was generous when it came to supporting good causes. He donated money for the new wing of the library, and they named it after his father. At the same time folks seemed to keep their distance from Jumbo. He never bothered most folks, but nobody really called him their friend.

At first I couldn't see who it was the other side of the marshy island. But then I heard that deep, low, growly voice again, and I knew I'd better sit tight. There was no mistaking it was Jumbo Rawlin.

I crouched down behind a tump of marsh grass and held on to two fistfuls of the wiry tough grass for dear life. I slipped the stern anchor into another tump, and it held. I lay flat in the bottom of the skiff, hoping and hoping Jumbo wouldn't come around the edge of the marsh and see me. Obie lay down beside me as if he understood perfectly what was going on. He made a space between his front paws and laid his chin there. The grass bowed and waved over our heads with the water's motion.

I couldn't get my heart to slow down and beat normal, and my breath came raggedy, but that was nothing compared to how I felt when I heard the outboard speed up and come nearer.

Jumbo was mumbling in an angry kind of way, and I could catch only a few phrases that got picked up by the breeze.

'Where you think you . . .' and 'I'll dump you so far out . . .' But most of what I heard was my heart in a deafening beat inside my head. Because the more Jumbo mumbled, the more I knew that I didn't want to hear a word of it.

When it sounded like Jumbo was right next to the skiff, I peeked over the gunwale. There he was, big as life, fishing around with his boathook, his back to me as he worked his way up the side of a smaller tump next to the one where I sat.

Don't panic, I said to myself, over and over. Don't panic, don't panic. Right beside the skiff was a small inlet that settled into the grass. I didn't know whether there was enough bottom for the skiff to get into it. I worked as quickly as my trembly-wild fingers would allow, letting out the anchor line and pushing the skiff with my hands along the edge of the grass. I eased us stern first into the opening, and was just hunkering down again as Jumbo turned to head out a little deeper.

The bottom of the skiff scraped on the marsh grass. I hoped we wouldn't get beached there with the tide going out, just me and Obie and the little crabs in the cold muck beneath us.

Then it occurred to me that Jumbo wouldn't bother with the backsides of those little tumps for long. Whatever he was looking for would be on its way out into the Bay on the retreating tide.

Eventually Jumbo followed the tide out, too. I pushed

us out of that little inlet, started the motor, and made for the opposite shore. We slipped around the mouth of the creek without coming to Jumbo's notice. Only then did my breathing start to sound normal.

It wasn't until later, after I'd met up with Tunes, that I began to wonder what in heaven's name Jumbo was looking for out there.

Chapter 2

The laughing gulls were swooping and swarming when I nosed the skiff in to the dock where Tunes waited with Kneebone. Doke had come in and was dumping the crabs that hadn't survived the catch. The gulls squabbled and dived at each other for the leavings.

Kneebone knelt down, his arthritic knees creaking, and took my painter in his gnarly hands. I handed him the string of fish I'd caught to put on ice and clean for supper. He took them without a word.

Kneebone had a reputation for being a grouch. Tunes and I knew his arthritis hurt him all the time. That was how he'd got his name. From the time he was teenager, her father's knees and elbows and knuckles were swollen and knobbly, like the limbs of an old apple tree.

It was worst when he was young, doing stoop labour. But Doc Wembly, who was doctor to a lot of the oldtimers on Virginia's Eastern Shore, had told Kneebone if there was solace to be taken, it was in knowing that having to work hard all his life, despite the pain, had kept him from being a lot worse off than he was. That happened to folks with arthritis who had a choice about what they did, and did nothing because everything hurt so bad.

Kneebone's painful joints made him the best weatherman around, and he had a natural feel for what the crops'd do. He'd installed all the irrigation equipment on the farm and knew how to fix and service it, as well as the tractors and harvesters and such. Dad said there wasn't a finer farmer alive than Kneebone.

Tunes busied herself getting her gear out of the truck. She and Kneebone didn't say anything. Tunes was silent as Kneebone most times, except when she and I were together and nobody else was around. It added to her mystery. Some folks said it came from living alone with her daddy in their weathered clapboard house. It might've been, but it also could've been Tunes was born that way, just like her daddy.

Tunes never spoke a word until she was three. Mama and Gran thought she just wasn't ready to talk, but some folks said she was dim-witted. Then one day shortly after her third birthday, she climbed up on her granddaddy's lap. He was a jolly old man who loved to sing and talk, unlike Kneebone, his son. Tunes had her granddaddy's mouth organ in her fat little hand, and she handed it to him.

'Play me some tunes, Granddaddy,' she said. It was the first thing she ever did say, and she'd parsed her words out one by one ever since, never wasting a breath. The name has stuck with her.

Some folks feel menaced by silence, and spend a good deal of time moving their jaws in an effort to avoid it. But I've grown up with Kneebone and Tunes and their quiet, serious way of being that doesn't depend on words. It's more comfortable to me than useless conversation.

Tunes wore blue jeans and a sweatshirt. She scrambled around handing things down into the skiff – a jug of water and a chest of ice, some apples, then the wide clamming rake and bushel baskets. She wore gum boots like mine, but she moved in and out of the boat graceful as a falcon, and looked as fierce as one, too, her gold-and-black eyes snapping, not missing a rock of the boat. Nobody said a word while Kneebone held on to the painter and Tunes stowed things in the locker under the stern seat before we shoved off.

'I want you young'uns in 'fore the sun heads on down.' Kneebone said as he cast us off. 'Hear?' We nodded, and he waved us on our way.

'Hey,' Tunes said as we headed out the inlet toward the mouth of the creek where the cherrystones lay buried in the sandbanks. She held up her hand and I slapped her five.

'Hey yourself,' I said.

Soon's we had a skiff-length of water between us 'n' the dock, she threw back her head and laughed.

'Hoo, hoo, hoo, hoo, hoo!' she shouted, her face split wide in a grin. 'I felt like one of those road men from the prison. We cleared roots with our bare hands, ploughed and hoed manure into the ground, and Kneebone had me sweeping and dusting – I sure am glad to see the back of Saturday morning!' She held up her hands. They were rough and cracked, and her fingernails were split and jagged.

'I sure missed you out fishing,' I said, then couldn't resist a brag. 'Had to let loose of more fish than I kept, and left the holes hotter'n I found 'em.'

'Well, good,' said Tunes, ' 'cause I told Kneebone we'd bring home a mess for supper tonight. Then he can give what you caught to Mazie.'

Her happiness infected me, and it was as fine a day for clamming as there ever would be. The storm Doke'd warned about never materialized, and the light was clear and bright and golden. Obie sat in the bow, the wind catching his ears and blowing them out like the wings of an aeroplane. He banked with the skiff as we sped through each turn of the channel.

The breeze was cool, but it felt like the first day of the first spring ever. The sun climbed and the air warmed, and the smells of brackish water, mud, fish and pine were set free from the cold that had locked them in all winter.

We laughed with the sheer joy of being alive and on the water. The sea nettles weren't in yet, and the water was extra-salty despite the rain we'd had. And icy cold. Obie jumped overboard every once in a while to cool off from the warm afternoon sun. I was just dead certain there wasn't a finer place on earth.

We clammed until our shoulders ached, dropping the rake into the green shallow water, and hauling it up full of muck and clams. Our feet and legs were numb from standing in the chilly water. The clams were big and plentiful. The sun danced on the water as if it was high summer. Skate soared by just beneath the surface like jet fighters on a mission, and nesting terns swooped us when we got too close to where they were making nests on the beaches. My, it was fine.

We ate our fill and packed two baskets with clams and eelgrass and ice from the chest before heading back up toward our farm on Pungotuck Creek, less than an hour's run.

As it was, we had a right good wind behind us, and the tide had turned and was heading back in, carrying us up the Bay at a good clip. When we got to the mouth of Little Creek, it suddenly reminded me of Jumbo.

I told Tunes what I'd seen. I slowed the boat to a near idle so I could talk, and Tunes' eyes got big and round.

'What was he lookin' for?' she asked.

'I don't know, but he sure was mad at somebody.'

'He's always mad, whether he has reason or not,' she said.

We were pretty near home, we'd had such a fine ride on the tide. We had more than an hour till sunset, so we headed up the creek a bit, content to glide and listen to the early birds just up from down South building their nests in tree branches that overhung the water. I cut the throttle, killing the engine, and we just drifted along with the tide.

We sailed toward a tump of marsh grass big as an island. A blue heron put up from where she waded, intent on the little silver flashes at the edge of the cordgrass. The heron nearly clipped us as she flew over, croaking and squawking in complaint at the interruption.

The boat quivered, and Obie, who was on point in the bow, gave a soft whine. He stood bent-legged, leaning forward to stare down into the bottle-green depth of the slow-moving channel as if to ask what I was waiting for. The salt had crusted into little white circles in the black fur around his nose, and the loose skin around his face and neck fell forward as he lowered his head to the spot where he wanted me to stop.

'There's no fish here next to the channel, Obie,' I said. 'Sun must'a got to you.' I looked at Tunes, who had been intent on fixing the tip of her new fishing pole. She looked up and wrinkled her nose, her expression clearly disdainful. Tunes took her fish-finding seriously, and she and Obie had a long-standing rivalry.

'Hmph,' she said. 'There's fish here and I'll eat bait.'

The whine in Obie's throat turned to a soft growl and he began dancing on the gunwales, leaning way forward, his nose just a few inches from the water. So I started the engine and turned the boat in a wide arc.

'It must be some right big lunker,' I muttered. 'Just hold your horses now.'

I got up even with him and had to shove him aside with my knee to get to where I could see. He kept crowding me. Tunes looked at him scornfully.

'What's the matter with you, Obie?' I had to nudge him aside again to get forward enough to find out what was putting the hair up on his neck.

Just below the surface was what looked at first like a large winter sea nettle, with fine brownish tentacles spreading out in a circle around it. Deeper down through the bottle-green murk I saw faintly a striped pattern of red, yellow and blue, like nothing in nature, rising and turning in slow motion, something from a dream.

It was a few moments before I realized I was seeing the first dead body I'd ever laid eyes on. I knew he was dead, 'cause if there was any air left in his lungs he'd 'a been floating up on the surface, not down a foot underwater. Dark green stripes of eelgrass had laced around the powerful arms.

'Tunes,' I said. 'Come here.' She looked up from rewrapping the eye at the tip of her fishing pole. 'Come here!'

I recognized something in the way the fingers curled gently downward, knew who it was the second I saw him. The hands were big, but even in death you could tell they were gentle hands, or had been.

'It's Jorge,' I said.

Tunes stood slowly, compelled by the quiet in my voice. But it was as if she didn't want to look, she moved so hesitant.

Jorge Rodrigues managed the teams of Mexican and Haitian labourers who came to the Eastern Shore in the spring and stayed through the harvest of strawberries, squash, cucumbers, peppers, potatoes, melons, apples, grapes, and anything else that needed picking through November.

Dad always said Jorge'd done wonderful things for the labourers, getting their housing improved and buses to take them to town and to church. And he was fair with the farmers, too, only asking for what was due and right. Tunes and me'd gone fishing with him since we were toddlers, sitting with him for hours in his boat, eating cheese sandwiches with pickle relish and drinking lemonade.

Something took over in my head, blocking my feelings like I was a trained policeman, and I looked around to mark in my mind the exact spot where we'd found him. Jorge had been real good to me all my life. But I never once let myself think about anything excepting how I'd be able to get him in to the dock safely.

I took the old sapling Dad had cut and stripped for me, a nail hammered in one end to catch the dock lines down at the landing, and stuck it down to feel the sticky mud bottom, then brought it up and carved a depth line with my pocket knife. And I looked up to see how the light lay pinkish at the horizon and estimated we had about a half hour till sunset.

Having done his job, Obie licked his chops and hunkered down in the middle of the boat, out of the way.

I gently hooked the nail at the end of the pole into the shirt bunched under Jorge Rodrigues's shoulder and drew him in next to the skiff. His skin looked as if the water had leached all the blood from him, leaving him a pale oystery colour, tinged grey where it should be brown, that forever after I would know as the colour of death.

Holding the sounding pole under one arm, I steered the idling motor over to the marsh at the edge of the creek.

I turned to Tunes. She just stood there, her arms out at near shoulder level, like she was balancing on a high wire, her breath all sucked in.

'Hold on to this so's I can get a line on him. We got to tow him back to the dock.'

Tunes looked at me like I was crazy. Without a word, she jumped over the gunwale. The chilly water poured over the tops of her rubber fishing boots, but she seemed not to notice or mind. She stood looking at me for a long moment over the angle of her shoulder. Then without a word she turned and slogged through the marsh, knee-deep in the thick marsh grass and sucking mud.

'Tunes, come back here! Where you going? Tunes, I need you!'

Her strides were long and purposeful. The water splashed up on her broad back and arms as she went, but she never broke stride. When she got to the top of the bank she turned once to look at me again for a long few seconds, the sun glinting off beads of water that had splashed on to her hair.

'I won't tell,' I shouted, but I had to swallow at the lump stuck in my gullet. She turned and was gone, like a deer in the twilit meadow.

I walked back slowly toward the stern, not changing the angle of the sapling pole so as not to dislodge Jorge, and managed somehow to get a line around his wrist. His skin felt strange and inanimate, like I was handling something made of soft, cool, rubbery clay. I cleated the line and started the motor again.

We made our way back slowly, the motor labouring mightily against the drag of Jorge's weight in the water, out to the Bay and up Pungotuck Creek, where the tide helped us in to Bartons' dock, which was a good half mile closer than our place.

At the time I was too shocked to wonder why Tunes had bolted like that, but I figured she had her reasons. Tunes always went to great lengths to avoid trouble. It was one of those quirks about her. As low-key a character as she was, she was always afraid attention would focus on her, and she'd do anything to avoid that.

I'd made up my mind without really thinking on it that I wouldn't even tell Dad Tunes was with me when I found Jorge. I'd say I let her off to walk back. Sometimes she did that. And if somehow it came out later that she was in the skiff, well, I'd deal with it then.

Chapter 3

I was grateful Judge Wickham was down on the dock when I landed. Kneebone was there, too, standing up behind the dock office alongside his truck. Kneebone had eyes like an eagle, and once he saw Tunes wasn't with me he watched closely what transpired. When he saw I was towing something large and heavy behind the skiff, he climbed into the cab and drove away. He didn't even stay to find out what had happened. Tunes got her aversion to trouble from her daddy.

There was an understanding between Kneebone and Tunes. He'd brought her up knowing right from wrong. He'd taught her how to take care of herself and to avoid trouble when she could. If she wasn't in the skiff with me, he figured she had her reasons, and that was that.

Judge stood up when he saw me come in. He, too, knew right off something was wrong. The engine laboured, and the skiff was low in the water. Despite her slow progress, she put out a wake that nudged fishing boats into the pilings all along the creek.

'What you got there, Buck?' Judge asked, his hand stroking his white-bristled chin.

'Oh, Judge! You got to help me!' I'd been so calm up till then the desperation in my voice surprised me. 'I got Jorge here. He's dead.'

Judge jammed his old khaki fishing hat down on his head and bent to take my painter, securing it to the dock. Then he climbed down into the skiff and uncleated the hauling line. For a man of eighty years he was agile as a

21

cat. Judge drew the body in beside the boat slowly and gently. I knew the man on the end of that line had been a friend as dear to the Judge as he had been to me and Tunes.

The memory of the last time I saw Jorge alive flashed through my mind. He and Tunes and I had been out fishing in Jorge's boat when we came upon Judge's old wooden scow hung up on a sandbar. Judge was panicked, rushing from gunwale to gunwale, peering into the swiftly moving water. We came alongside, and Judge was right glad to see us.

'This shoal just appeared from nowheres,' Judge said. He looked indignant but hesitant and confused. That shoal had always been there, a red marker at either end. None of us said a word. We towed Judge home. By the time we got down to Church Creek, Judge was his old self again. It was just like Jorge not to pay Judge's spells any mind. Judge always came around right again. But Jorge worried about him going out on the Bay alone.

'Oh, dear, dear Lord,' Judge said, soon's he saw Jorge. 'How could this've happened?' It wasn't a question, really, more an expression of dismay.

'Where'd you find him, son?' Judge asked, and I told him. To my horror, I was fighting tears and couldn't say any more.

Up until that moment I'd concentrated intently on doing my job as well as I could. Thinking of everything Sheriff would ask me, trying to take note of every detail, and getting Jorge in to the dock took all of my energy and attention. It had kept me from thinking about Jorge.

It didn't seem possible he was gone, with his arms and legs and the rest of his body still right there. I couldn't imagine Jorge having an accident. He didn't look like a natural athlete with his broad shoulders, barrel chest, and short legs. But he listened and watched carefully and thought seriously before he moved or spoke. Low to the ground as he was, his actions were always true as his words.

I must have stood there a full minute without moving, thinking about Jorge, while Judge secured the skiff and looked out over the stern at the body. I thought of Jorge's gentle little wife and his two daughters, who were a year and two years behind Tunes and me in school. They'd never again see him smile so wide his eyes'd disappear. I felt my face crumple, and Judge put his arm around my shoulders and held me against him, never letting go of the line tied to Jorge's wrist.

'Well, Buck, you did good to get him in here,' Judge said. His eyes filled with tears, and he clapped his hand on my shoulder. 'Climb up and holler for Doke. Tell him to call Sheriff.'

Well, Doke came, Sheriff came, and most everybody else in Sheriff's office. Pretty soon everyone on the creek was there, just to have a look at Jorge before the light faded.

Doke and Evie Barton helped Judge haul Jorge from the water. His left temple was stove in, like a half-gone melon, and a tiny neat red hole sat in the centre of his forehead like a beauty mark. His eyes were open in a watery lifeless stare, and I was incredulous that Jorge was gone from behind them. I was scared and suddenly felt as if I might be sick.

'How could this happen?' Judge asked softly, of no one in particular. 'Who could've done such a thing?' Judge wiped the back of his hand across his mouth.

I turned and ran down the dock, to or from what, I didn't know. But I knew beyond doubt that Jorge's death had not been any accident, and I had a good idea who would have done such a thing. Jumbo Rawlin had been up to no good that morning, and I'd known it from the moment I'd seen him. Fear spread through me like I'd swallowed a powerful potion.

Dad was just walking down the ramp to the dock from his pickup. He caught me and held me like a little kid. I was shaken so badly I didn't mind a bit. I clamped on to him with my arms and legs and let him hold me close.

By dark it seemed all of Northampton County was there, farmers and watermen alike, milling around their pickup trucks outside the dock office, scratching their heads and talking low, the smoke from their cigarettes curling in the headlamps.

Doc Wembly heard the call at the hospital, where he was on his evening rounds, and came down to the dock just ahead of the ambulance. Doc looked Jorge over while the medics were getting out the stretcher and a body bag. Sheriff questioned me, and Deputy Jones took notes by flashlight.

The two medics, the Marsden brothers, Charlie and Bryce, lifted him like you'd lift a roll of tar paper, not being careful of him as they laid him on top of the unzipped bag. Bryce accidentally stepped on Jorge's hand, which had fallen off his chest.

I wanted to say be careful, be gentle, you'll hurt him. But of course that was ridiculous. Jorge couldn't feel anything any more. They took him off without sirens, just the red lights flashing, and that was that.

I told Sheriff everything, save two things. I didn't say Tunes had been with me. I didn't see that my telling would've made any difference. I also didn't tell about seeing Jumbo fishing around with his boathook earlier in the day, cursing in his skiff. I felt sure Jumbo'd killed Jorge, and somehow the body'd got away from him, and that's what he was looking for out among the islands of marsh grass. Why he might have killed Jorge, I didn't know.

Sheriff didn't say anything when we'd finished, just walked back and forth on the dock, rubbing at the back of his neck, muttering to himself. Sheriff was a big man, solid and comfortable-looking. I was to learn soon how his size could menace you if you were the object of his suspicion.

Anxious as I was to put Sheriff on the right track to catching whoever'd killed Jorge, I was terrified of what Jumbo might do to me for telling about him being out poking around with his boathook.

It was after nine o'clock when Dad and I headed home from Sheriff's office in Eastville, the vapour rising from the swamps either side of the road. I wanted to tell Dad about Jumbo, but I didn't know how to begin. About halfway home I just blurted it out.

'I got to tell you something, Dad!' He slowed the truck and looked over at me. 'I saw something right strange this morning.'

Dad stopped the truck and pulled off the county road onto a dirt track. He turned to listen to me, his arm along the back of the seat behind my head. The dashboard lights reflected off his eyes and nose and chin line in a ghosty green outline.

When I'd finished, Dad let his breath out real slow.

'Why didn't you tell Sheriff that before?' he asked.

'Well, I know I'm not supposed to be there around Jumbo's property, and – '

'Buck, that's no reason, and you know it.' He put the truck into gear and pulled back out onto the county road.

'I was afraid Sheriff wouldn't believe me,' I said.

'Well, I'm sure there's some explanation for what Mr Rawlin was doing out there,' Dad said. 'He could've been looking for anything.'

Right then I sure wished I'd told Dad about Jumbo shooting at Tunes and me the fall before. It would have laid out some of Jumbo's violent history.

I thought about how, impossible as it was to keep a secret on the Eastern Shore, some things folks never talked about seemed to be the darkest secrets of all. Like Jumbo – his meanness, his tendency toward drunken violence, his racial prejudice, his fear of dogs and hatred of children. What folks talked about when it came to Jumbo was his public-spirited generosity. Worst anybody ever said about him was that he was peculiar.

That grownups couldn't see how evil Jumbo was only added to his aura, far's Tunes and me were concerned. We reckoned they feared him, too, only they just didn't recognize it, as if he'd cast a spell over them.

The night was clear and lit by the moon. Dad was one to play it by the book, and I was surprised he didn't take me straight on back to Sheriff's office.

Mama and Gran were waiting to hear from us what-all had happened. They were at the kitchen table, Mama in her long white apron over her white blouse and slim grey skirt, kneading bread dough. Her glasses had slipped clear down to the end of her nose, and unruly red curls blossomed out around her freckled face.

Mama wasn't one for putting words to feelings. But you could pretty much tell what to expect when you came in and smelled what was cooking. She always made bread when she was nervous, cakes when she was happy, and she fried chicken when she was mad.

Mama looked up when we came in.

'There's stew in the oven,' she said, and went back to her kneading. Her long slim hands were covered with flour up above her wrists. 'You must be starving.'

Gran was embroidering a sheet in a little hoop, the rest of it spread out across her lap.

Soon's we came into the kitchen, Obie went over to his corner behind the stove, let himself fall so that you could hear each and every bone hit the floor, curled up on his old rug, and went straight to sleep. I had a powerful urge to do the same, mostly in the hope that when I woke up I'd find it had been just a nightmare that never happened at all.

Dad went straight to the phone and rang Sheriff's office. He had to wait a long time to talk to Sheriff, and meantime Gran looked at me with her piercing blue eyes. A soft halo of white hair framed her face. To look at her, you'd think she was all sweetness and light, which is what Granddaddy used to call her. But if ever there was a woman of steel, it was Gran.

'Tell us what happened, Buck,' she said.

'Well,' I began, taking a deep breath. 'Me and Tunes was –'

'Tunes and I were,' Mama interrupted.

'For pity's sake, Jen,' said Gran, 'let him tell it!'

Mama pushed her glasses back up her nose with her wrist, leaving a smudge of flour on her cheek. 'Go on,' she said.

'Tunes and I were coming back up the creek,' I said, picking my words carefully. 'She said she wanted to walk home, so I let her out just below Little Neck . . .'

When I'd provided enough details about finding Jorge to satisfy them a bit, Dad was finished on the phone.

'Sheriff says to come on back down,' he said. Mama and Gran looked at each other without speaking. 'Buck hasn't told Sheriff everything,' he said. He repeated what I'd said on the way home, about seeing Jumbo and all.

'Dear Lord,' was what Gran said. Mama stood there peeling dough off her cuticles. Her face was pale as the flour on the kneading board, showing off every freckle.

'You go on to bed,' Dad said to them. 'I'm not hungry. How about you? You'd better eat something.'

I shook my head no.

'Chances are there's an explanation why Jumbo was out there this morning,' Dad said. 'But Sheriff wants to know everything that might pertain to the investigation.'

Dad and I got back in the truck and drove down to Eastville, where Sheriff waited for us.

When we'd talked before, Sheriff had been right kindly, telling me he couldn't wait till I finished school so he could hire me, I'd been so careful with my facts and details and all.

Now he stood with his thumbs hooked into his belt loops, wrists turned out and shoulders hunched forward, like something was eating on him terrible.

'Why didn't you tell me this before?' He looked worried and stern, and suddenly my stomach turned sour. I looked at Dad, but he wasn't going to help me out.

'Well, sir,' I said hoarsely, my throat closing up on me again, and tears threatening at the back of my eyes. The night was chilly, and I wanted to fly out into the darkness, headed for somewhere far away, with the bats and coons in the mist, into a back creek where nobody would find me.

'Go on, son,' Dad said, nudging my shoulder from behind.

'It's because I was afraid.' I was ashamed to say that, but once the words were out, there was no stopping more words coming.

'Jumbo . . . Mr Rawlin's not as nice a man as folks think he is.' I looked at Dad, who said nothing.

'How's that?' Sheriff asked.

He looked at Dad and sat down heavily in his old wooden swivel chair. He motioned Dad to sit in the straight-back chair by the side of the desk.

I rushed on, unable to stop now I'd started. 'He menaced Tunes and me once for . . . for coming too close to his property. And he beat up Mrs Rawlin real bad before she went away, so bad her eyes were swollen shut. I seen her. And he shot Kneebone's hound.'

My heart was beating so loudly I could barely hear. I'd almost given away the secret of the shooting incident. I'd gone too far, telling Sheriff about Kneebone's hound. Kneebone had told Dad that hound just disappeared one full-moon night when it seemed every bitch on the neck was in season. Few days later he washed up on the shore across the creek from Jumbo's with a .22 hole clear through his head. Everybody knew Jumbo walked his property with a .22 rifle in his hand. Never went on his rounds without it.

But nobody ever mentioned Jumbo Rawlin in connection with shootings or disappeared hounds. Kneebone and Tunes would not appreciate me bringing their names up in connection with trouble. But what was said was said, and I wasn't one hundred percent sorry, neither.

'Just because a man is gruff and doesn't want folks on his propity doesn't mean he'd kill a man,' Sheriff said, leaning forward in his chair so his face was just a few inches from mine. 'Mr Rawlin's done a lot of good for Northampton County. He donates fresh produce from his farm to the food bank for poor folks. He's sat on the County Board of Supervisors.' Sheriff paused.

'And another thing, shooting dogs that're running your propity is not illegal. But I appreciate your telling me, Buck. Fact is,' he went on, 'though Jorge died of a gunshot wound, somebody hit him right hard upside the head first. At this moment we have no motive, no suspect, and no weapon.'

The room was hot, but at the same time I felt all shivery. Everything seemed to have unnaturally sharp edges.

'You have no reason to be afraid of Jumbo Rawlin. He's right strange at times, but he doesn't mean anything personal against anyone. I don't believe he'd harm you.

'I'm going over to Mr Rawlin's in the morning to ask some questions. I have to tell him what you saw, but at the moment at least I don't have to tell who saw it. Let's just keep this amongst ourselves for the time being, all right?'

I nodded, and when I blew the air out of my lungs I felt like I'd been holding my breath for the whole time we'd been with Sheriff.

On the way home Dad was quiet for a few minutes, and I was thinking about going off to sleep.

'Buck, sometimes young'uns get to imagining things, especially with someone like Mr Rawlin being so odd. Perhaps he doesn't like kids. It doesn't mean he's likely to do something's bad as murder a man. And just because Jorge was kind to you and took you fishing doesn't mean he didn't do something that got him into trouble, maybe got him killed.'

'But, Dad, Jumbo . . . Mr Rawlin's always having trouble with labour. He tried to cheat the workers out of wages, and he wouldn't fix their roofs. Those shacks are filthy and full of bugs. Jorge and Mr Rawlin argued about it – everybody knows that!'

'Buck, I know you don't like Mr Rawlin. But there's no evidence whatever he's done anything illegal, not even keeping the labour camp poorly. Look at his own place – it's a mess. You don't have to like Mr Rawlin. But don't judge him in Jorge's death.

'Still,' Dad went on, 'I'm proud of the way you handled yourself today. It would have been better to tell Sheriff right off that you saw Mr Rawlin out there. Even when you're afraid, it's always better to follow your instincts and tell the truth. Understand?'

'Yessir,' I said. I wanted to tell him that every one of my instincts had been screaming at me *not* to tell Sheriff about Jumbo, and they hadn't begun to quiet down at all, now I'd told. But knowing how Dad felt about the truth and that I still kept from Sheriff and him that Tunes had been with me burned a hole in my chest.

I knew that was the end of talk about Jumbo, but even after seeing how Sheriff looked all doubtful when I told him what I'd seen, I was surer'n a hot humid summer that Jumbo had done Jorge in, and I was filled with foreboding at what might happen next.

Chapter 4

Sunday morning I woke wishing again I'd dreamed it all. But when I saw my jeans and shirt on the chair at the end of my bed splashed with bottom muck from the Bay, everything came tumbling back, detail by detail.

My first thought was of Jorge's misshapen head, and then I thought of Sheriff and all his questions. I had a huge sickening lump in my stomach.

I heard noises in the kitchen below. I threw my legs over the side of the bed and they touched Obie, who lay curled on the carpet, his nose tucked among his paws, still sound asleep.

'Wake up, boy,' I said softly, shaking his back with my feet. 'If you think I'm going through this day by myself, you're crazy!' He stretched his legs out in front of him, arched his back like a cat, yawned loudly, and went back to sleep.

I hopped over him and slipped into clean jeans and shirt. I felt headachy and disoriented. Obie must have felt the same way. I had to yank on him for almost a full minute while he groaned and whined, and finally he got to his feet, stiff as an arthritic old horse.

Downstairs in the kitchen, nobody said anything apart from good morning. Mama wore a new bright blue dress with big gold buttons and matching high heels. She put a stack of Gran's streaming corn pancakes in front of me.

'We goin' to church?' I asked.

'Are we *going* to church?' Mama said, correcting me. 'Well, of course! The sooner things get back to normal around here, the better I'll like it. Eat your breakfast.' Mama liked things to be normal. She busied herself getting me another stack of pancakes. The phone rang.

'Well, hello, Delia!' Mama said. It was her friend Mrs Thales from the garden club. I wondered if Mama felt as chirpy as she looked – like a nervous bird, hands all fluttery and eyes so bright. 'Oh,' she said. 'Why, it's just terrible . . . Buck's fine. Yes . . .We're so proud of him . . . He's been so brave . . .' She winked at me. My stomach sank even lower, and I pushed a wedge of sticky pancake around on my plate.

Those corn pancakes, normally my favourite, especially with Gran's blueberry preserves, appealed to me about as much as wood chips.

Yesterday, when I was so tired and shocked at what-all had happened, everything was bigger than life. Today the world and its contents seemed smaller and too sharply focused to be real, like I was looking through the wrong end of a telescope.

The kitchen was filled with the smell of baking, and sunlight bounced everywhere. Even the bare wood table gleamed beneath my plate. Right there, in the place that'd given me so much comfort, a strange feeling began to slither around in me. I wondered whether things would ever return to normal, and if something inside me hadn't changed for all time.

I'd never not told the truth before. Even when Tunes 'n' me stole Gran's apple pie from the back-kitchen windowsill I never hesitated a second when Dad asked if we'd done it. Knowing full well I'd get a tanning and not be able to go fishing for a week – it turned out to be two – I said, 'Yessir, I thought it was a good idea at the time, seein' as how I was going to end up eating most of it anyways.'

The truth was a big issue in our family. But then I'd never had as good a reason not to tell it before. Going back on my word to Tunes was far worse than not telling she'd been with me when I found Jorge, and it seemed to me she needed protecting. Nonetheless I felt awful.

Obie sat beneath the table, hoping something would drop. I slipped him two pancakes and his tail whumped, causing Gran to turn from the sink and arch an eyebrow at me. It wasn't like me not to eat her corn pancakes.

I was saved from embarrassment by Sheriff, who chose that moment to drop by. He tapped lightly on the kitchen screen door.

'Mornin', Senior. Jen, Miz Smith, Buck,' Sheriff said through the screen, tipping his hat to Mama and Gran. 'Senior, I was wondering if you and Buck would come down to my office after church.'

A puff of rosemary-scented breeze wafted through the screen. Dad stood and reached for his hat. Instead of inviting Sheriff in, he went outside, pulling the heavy wooden door behind him. Obie squeezed past his knees and headed down to the creek for his morning swim before Dad could get the door shut.

Through the rippled windowpanes I watched Dad and Sheriff, standing shoulder to shoulder on the brick path that crisscrossed the herb garden. Dad listened, his head bent, and Sheriff talked, all the while rubbing at the back of his neck.

'Son, where's Tunes?' Dad asked when he came back in, closing the screen door behind him and leaving the wooden door open. My heart leapt into my mouth again.

Gran and Mama bustled around washing up in time to leave for church.

'I don't know, sir,' I said, struggling to keep my voice normal. Cat had scooted in between his feet and the door, and she rubbed up against my leg. I bent to pick her up and scratched her ears, trying to appear calm. 'I haven't seen her since yesterday.'

'Sheriff wants her and Kneebone to come with us when we go to his office after church. Take your bike over and ask them to meet us downtown around one o'clock. Hurry now, we'll be late to church.'

I was grateful for the chance to get away before he guessed I was having a hard time keeping myself together. The only reason I could think of for Sheriff wanting to see them was that someone – Jumbo, most likely – saw Tunes and me out on the creek together – around the time we found Jorge.

I hated to think of how Tunes' face would look when Sheriff confronted us. I'd seen it many times before: a hardening around her eyes and mouth, a kind of knowing she'd been blamed for something she hadn't done.

I called Obie, who came up dripping from the creek. He was happy to be going somewhere, didn't matter where, and ran ahead of my bicycle down the sandy track to Kneebone's house. Wild dogwood hung over the road. Every year the swollen dogwood buds spilling out their snowy round petals filled me with inexpressible joy. But that day I felt sick and depressed. How things could change in no time at all!

I skidded around the last bend in the track and pulled into the front yard of the weathered clapboard house where Tunes and Kneebone lived.

Kneebone kept the two-storeyed house in good repair and spotless-clean. Any time a board rotted out he'd poke through the scrap lumber up behind the packing shed and find just the right size to replace it. The boards showed a history of paint – the newest ones were fairly white. The originals were a soft grey with little grooves of white in the grain.

The house was in the woods, where jonquils that had gone wild still glimmered in the tree-filtered light. And here and there peonies arched, a brilliant pink aching to burst out from the buds. The perfume of the untended lilacs wafted through the woods. Tunes' mama had planted the flowers some fourteen years before when she was Kneebone's bride, fresh from Carolina. But nobody had tended them since she'd died. In summer Tunes and Kneebone kept a little vegetable patch, with okra and cabbage, greens and beans.

Everything about Tunes and Kneebone's house appealed to me – reminded me of the two of them, how straightforward they were. There were no frills and nothing in it that didn't have a good practical use. Our house seemed fussy by comparison, probably because I had to do so much yard work, and help Mama and Gran clean weekends when I could have been fishing.

Kneebone's old bitch came crawling out from under the house to greet Obie, head down and showing her teeth in a grin. She was a skinny, mangy thing who looked just a step from the grave. The sight of Obie lifted her spirits, and she galloped around like a puppy, her back end tucked under, enticing him to play.

'Tunes!' I called as I laid my bicycle up against a loblolly pine near the front steps. 'Kneebone!' His green pickup truck was there by the front stoop, polished and shiny to belie the fifteen years he'd been bumping all over the farm in it.

I banged loudly on the door. 'Anybody home?' There was no answer. I tried the knob, and the door swung wide into the kitchen. The dishes were stacked neatly on their rims in the drainer. The sun sparkled in between the blue-and-white checkered curtains. The garbage had been emptied, and a clean brown paper grocery bag lined the trash can in the corner. The worn wooden floorboards were swept and polished.

'Tunes! Kneebone! Where are you?' The house was still except for the plastic battery clock clicking softly over the white porcelain sink and a squirrel scratching on the tin roof. I reached out gingerly with one hand to feel if the cast-iron stove was still hot from breakfast, but it was cold. They'd either gotten up good and early or skipped breakfast.

I wondered if Kneebone's sister Mazie might have come by to take them to her house for breakfast and persuade them to go to church. Mazie and her husband, Jep, went to the New Bethel AME church every Sunday at ten o'clock.

Kneebone and Tunes rarely went to church. It wasn't that they didn't believe. It was rather that they didn't much hold with anyone telling them what and how they should believe. And they took their meditations into the woods and fields and out on to the creeks, where they could be worshipful before all creation. I was of the same mind, but Mama and Gran would never let me spend a Sunday morning anywhere but at Hungars Episcopal church, one of the oldest in Virginia.

Mama, Gran, Dad and I passed by New Bethel on our way to Hungars that morning. Mazie's car wasn't there. It was early, and Dad said we'd come back after services were over.

Our church was a stout brick building. We sat in the pew we always sat in. The sun shone in through the polished windows, burnishing the brass and making the vases of tulips on the altar glow like they had haloes.

Walking up the church aisle just forward of where I sat between Mama and Gran, Jumbo Rawlin was showing Miz Thales to her pew. His long arms stuck out from his jacket sleeves, leaving an inch of wrist uncovered. He was sun- and windburned everywhere, save behind his ears and a line on the back of his neck where he'd just had a haircut. A little twitch of fear wiggled somewhere behind my breastbone just at the sight of him.

Jumbo bobbed his head at various neighbours as he returned to usher in another parishioner. Folks on both sides of the aisle nodded back and smiled what seemed then like respectful little smiles for an exemplary, Godfearing citizen. Now it occurs to me they were smiles of folks who just didn't quite know what to make of Jumbo Rawlin.

I was grateful for the sermon, of which I heard not a word, because it gave me a chance to think about Tunes and me fishing – like we'd done just yesterday. That had a calming effect on me. I went through church like a robot. I stood and sat and knelt and said the words automatically.

Afterward, at the coffee hour in the parish house, men dressed in tweed jackets and red-striped ties and women wearing high heels and perfume patted me on the shoulder and bent over to whisper in my ear what a good job I'd done, they were so proud of me keeping my wits in all the excitement, being so helpful to Sheriff, how proud Mama and Dad must be.

Jumbo made his way among the churchgoers. I was aware of where he was every second, as if radar set a small spot between my shoulder blades to jumping every time he passed close by, like he was a bumblebee threatening to sting. But he didn't speak to me or anybody else in the family. I was relieved when Dad came up behind me and said it was time to go.

We drove back up to New Bethel AME, where folks were just streaming out the front door. The women wore bright dresses and matching hats. The men wore coloured blazers with their hair all shiny and slicked back so you could still see the comb tracks. They looked like riotous bouquets of just-picked flowers.

But no Mazie, no Kneebone, no Tunes. So Dad and I took Mama and Gran home, then drove on down to Sheriff's office in Eastville.

It was a beautiful morning, golden with sunlight and breezy – the kind you'd think would lift the sorriest heart. I only noticed it in contrast to how I felt.

'Dad,' I said, when we were about halfway there, 'I got a strong feeling that Mr Rawlin is more than "peculiar", like folks say. What about him beating up Mrs Rawlin? And killing dogs? I got a terrible feeling about him, like he's evil, like he has no good to him at all. I don't understand why folks behave like he's the opposite of what he is.'

Dad went quiet for a moment.

'Evil's such a hard thing to identify, Buck. It's easy to mistake something completely different for it. Mr Rawlin's a rough man. He's graceless. Nobody knows for sure he beat Mrs Rawlin. He's uncomfortable inside his own skin, and maybe that's what you see, not necessarily evil.'

I thought about that all the way to Eastville, and wondered how my father, who was so thoughtful and so sure of himself, could be so wrong.

Sheriff and Deputy Jones were waiting in their office, the other side of the town square from the Eastern Shore Inn, where folks were gathering on the porch to go in for a pancake breakfast.

Well, I was right about one thing. Jumbo had denied any involvement in Jorge's death. But he was smarter than I gave him credit for. When Sheriff'd gone out to the Rawlin place to question him early Sunday, Jumbo said he'd been out Saturday fishing around the marshes with his boathook all right – it was off his own property, after all.

Said he was looking for an antique wooden hunting skiff he'd chained to his dock and filled with water until the gunwales just hovered below the surface. Antique boats and guns were Jumbo's hobby, and he was trying to swell the skiff's planks so it'd be bayworthy again. Said he was going to restore it.

Further, he claimed somebody had cut the chain and emptied out the skiff so it had wandered off on the tide. And he'd produced the ruined skiff *and* the cut chain for Sheriff's benefit.

When Sheriff asked why he'd bothered to chain the skiff, when folks around here never secured their boats with more'n a rope, Jumbo said somebody'd been stealing stuff lately from his house and his truck.

Worse, he said Tunes an' me were always skulking around his property, and he'd seen us out on the creek near his farm the day Jorge was found. Said he'd suspected we were the ones who cut the chain on his skiff. Which, incidentally, he said, he was fixin' to donate to the new watermen's museum down in Cape Charles. Said I was obsessed with getting even since Mama and Dad had a peck of worries on his account. Jumbo'd sold off land on the neck to developers, and our taxes went so high we had to sell off land to pay them. And that was true enough.

'Buck, do you know anything about Mr Rawlin's skiff?' Sheriff asked.

As filled with worry and grief as I'd been, suddenly the only thing in my heart was hatred. It filled me so full I felt I would burst. That Jumbo could turn things around so it looked like me 'n' Tunes'd done something wrong was not only clever of him but flat-out evil genius.

'No, sir,' I managed to say. 'He's plain and simple lying.' I meant to go on, but I couldn't get my breath. 'He's lying!'

'Well, I saw the skiff and the cut chain myself,' Sheriff said. 'What do you know about Tunes and Jorge?'

Sheriff saw I was having a hard time getting myself under control. 'Take your time, Buck,' he said. I took a few deep breaths and then answered.

'We were both friends with him, Tunes no more'n me,' I said. 'Well, he took us out fishing on the Bay when the water was too rough for my skiff, and . . .'

But I could see that was not what Sheriff meant. There was a long silence, and I looked from Sheriff to Deputy Jones to Dad and back to Sheriff.

'What exactly do you mean?' I asked.

'Mr Rawlin said there was some kind of . . . uh – romance between Tunes and Jorge.'

'No!' I said, and then I lost it. 'He's a lyin' snake. Tunes wouldn't . . .' I paused again to catch my breath. 'Jorge was a grown man with a family. He would never . . .'

'Was Tunes in the boat with you yesterday when you found Jorge?' Sheriff asked. My heart lurched. Dad put his hand on my shoulder, like a reminder of his lecture about telling the truth. I figured they'd soon get to the bottom anyways, and Tunes might get blamed worse if I didn't get it out in the open right then. With enormous effort, I kept ahold of my runaway heart.

'Yessir,' I said softly. 'But she wasn't with me when I saw Mr Rawlin out there with his boathook. And I never knew a thing about his skiff, nor did Tunes – '

'Buck, why didn't you tell me Tunes was with you in the first place? Now I don't know what to believe about everything you've told me. Did she make you promise?'

'Sir,' I began, but I was too upset to make sense of what I wanted to say. And suddenly it all seemed terribly complicated. 'Tunes didn't ask me not to tell. You know how she is, real private, keeps to herself. I knew without her saying she didn't want me to tell she was with me. Soon's we found Jorge's body, she jumped out of the skiff and waded ashore. She stopped at the edge of the marsh and I swore to her I wouldn't say she was in the skiff. I haven't seen her since. I swear that's the truth. I didn't want to go back on my word, is all. Tunes is my best friend.'

'Okay, Buck, I want you to listen real careful to what I ask you now, and think real hard before you answer. It's important you tell the exact truth. Was Tunes with Jorge Friday night?'

'No, sir,' I answered immediately. 'Kneebone had her on a short tether 'cause she caught over the limit fishing last week. She wasn't allowed out until Saturday morning.'

Sheriff cut his eyes over to Dad. I didn't like the way the silence hung among us.

'Why?' I asked. 'I know she wasn't with Jorge,' I blurted out. 'Kneebone didn't know it, but she and I were out dipping for bait. Then she baby-sat Mazie's grandbabies.'

I don't know now what possessed me. The part about netting bait wasn't even a half-truth. We'd gone the day before, not that evening. But it had come out before I could stop it. I just hated hearing Sheriff say anything bad about her. And I knew she hadn't done anything wrong.

'You'd best be sure, Buck,' Sheriff said. 'Because Mr Rawlin said he saw them headed down the dirt track behind the labour camp. They were arguing, and Jorge pushed her and hit her. It's the last anybody saw him before he was killed.'

'No!' I said. 'Jorge would never hit Tunes! Can't you see? He's trying to make it look like Tunes did it. I know – knew – Jorge, and I know Tunes better'n anybody, and there wasn't anything like that between them. I'm positive. That Mr Rawlin's a lyin' snake!'

'Well, I'm looking to question her,' Sheriff said. 'And you'd best stay out of the way. Hear?'

I nodded dumbly.

Chapter 5

On the way back from Sheriff's, Dad was right grim. And I was numb.

'Son,' he said, 'I thought you'd learned a lesson about honesty.'

'Yessir,' I said, 'I did.' But I knew what was coming. And I wasn't up to saying much, because I knew how deep in trouble Tunes was. And she didn't even know it.

'You had the chance then to say Tunes was with you out on the creek. Sheriff's right. Even I wonder – what else haven't you told us?'

'Nothing, sir,' I said. 'I swear on the Bible.' There was a silence from the driver's seat. 'You know I'd never swear on the Bible –'

'Now I have to wait and see if anything else turns up to prove you're not telling the truth,' said Dad, deflating me like he was a pin. He opened and closed his grip on the steering wheel. 'That's what lyin' does, son. Plants the kernel of distrust. Understand?'

'Yessir,' I said. Dad was also worried I'd be implicated, I guessed, but still. He knew Tunes well enough to understand why I'd lied.

'Dad, isn't there ever a good reason – your best friend – to lie?'

'When we get home, Buck, I want you to padlock the skiff and bring me the key.'

'Is there, Dad?'

'I don't want you out on the water again until I say so. I know that'll be right tough on you, but punishment's not meant to be easy – '

'Dad, answer me!'

'Stop trying to get out of this. I don't want you involved any further than you already are. Hear?' His face was dark with an anger that made no sense to me.

'Yessir,' I said again. I was mad as heck, but I knew I wouldn't get anywhere with him.

I was confused. Surely he understood my point of view, even if he didn't agree with me. But why was he so angry? It must have been fear, was all I could think.

But I urgently needed to get to Tunes and let her know Jumbo was trying to set her up.

Dad and I were both silent the rest of the way home.

I waited until Dad had set out for the packing shed and Mama and Gran had started getting Sunday dinner ready – roast chicken, mashed potatoes, peas, carrots, ham, okra, iced tea and apple pie, which usually was my favourite meal – and bicycled back over to Tunes' house.

I pedalled so fast I skidded around the curves and corners of the sandy track, sending up a dove and, a piece farther on, some partridges. Most times my heart would've taken off with those partridges' fat little brown bodies. But that day I hardly took notice of their flight. Obie was hard pressed to keep up with me, coming up behind, his tongue hanging to his knees.

I had to warn Tunes and Kneebone it was no longer a case of being afraid Tunes'd be blamed for something she didn't do. If we couldn't prove she didn't kill Jorge, I was afraid she'd go to jail. I hated the thought of Sheriff out looking for her.

I could tell when I came around the last bend, by the way the curtains hung forlorn in the windows, nobody was home, although they had been. Kneebone's truck was gone. For some reason, so were his dogs.

Obie and I checked out the house, then wheeled the bicycle around back just to see if we'd missed something. We sat on the back stoop for a few minutes, looking into the woods in the vague hope they'd come back and everything would be okay.

A flock of cardinals lit in a bittersweet bush that'd been red with berries before they arrived, and then was red with fat birds after. They must have just then come from farther south. As if one of them gave a signal, they flew in the same instant into the woods and were gone.

I was about to get back on my bicycle and pedal home when I heard a truck grinding through the sandy track leading the back way in from the main road.

I sat there as if glued to the step, trying to think just how to tell Tunes and Kneebone what-all had happened with Sheriff and what I was afraid it meant. Obie sat by my knee, panting in the watery sunlight that shone down through branches that were tinted green with buds. He looked over his shoulder without interest toward the truck. His head sagged and his eyes drooped. It was time for his midafternoon nap.

Kneebone's truck pulled up to the house, and both doors opened. I didn't have any intention of eavesdropping, I'd only paused there for a moment. I knew they were going to be right unhappy about what I had to say.

Then I heard Mazie's husband, Jep, say, 'Get your stuff, now, we'll wait here. Be quick.' Jep was a big, muscular man with a quick temper and a deep anger. His sharp voice made me stay right where I was. I didn't want to talk to Kneebone and Tunes in front of Jep. The screen door thwacked, and light, quick footsteps over my head sounded like Tunes running upstairs.

Just then a second car came chugging in from the opposite direction, crunching over the oyster-shell drive and sending up showers of grey, powdery dust. Another car door opened and closed. All I could think was that it was Sheriff coming to get Tunes. But the car sounded big and old, with a jitter to the body and a tic to the motor – not like the powerful four-by-four wagon Sheriff drove.

I got down and looked under the house to see who it was, but all I could see was ankles and feet. I ducked my head and slithered under the house, pushing curtains of old cobwebs in front of me, chicken and rabbit bones the dogs had dragged in with them cutting into my elbows and knees as I crawled through the sandy soil. I looked back over my shoulder just as Obie pulled himself in after me and sank beside one of the cinder-block footings that held the house two feet off the ground, and gave himself over to sleep.

By lying out flat behind the front steps and resting my cheek on my hands I could see them, Mazie, Jep and Kneebone, standing beside Kneebone's truck. They looked tired and stricken, as if they'd been up all night. Jep wore jeans and a sweatshirt with a clenched black fist on the front. Mazie wore a housedress, a large grey woollen cardigan and an apron, and old tennis shoes with no laces. She looked like a female Kneebone, with fine features, short greying hair and slender, sinewy arms and legs.

A very large black man wearing a seersucker suit lumbered toward them through the clearing, away from a late-sixties-model yellow sedan.

'Why it's the Reverend King Saloman Jones!' Mazie said, in her voice a mix of respect, scorn and disbelief. Many's the time I'd heard Tunes and Kneebone and Mazie talk about the Reverend King Saloman Jones of the New Bethel AME church, and how he was always interfering in folks' private business, not 'minding his flock', as Mazie put it, sticking his nose where it hadn't ought to be. Jep liked him because he stood up for black folks in the community.

The Reverend was right unpopular in the white churches, because folks saw him as a troublemaker. Every time there was an event or a speaker in Richmond the Reverend King Saloman Jones was marshalling his forces, organizing busloads of black folks to go there, when sometimes nobody had any idea what it was all about.

Jep rushed over and embraced the Reverend, who sweated profusely over a white clerical collar despite the cool breeze. Mazie shook his hand, making a funny little curtsy as she did.

'What brings you here, Reverend?' Jep asked. His face held a smile, but his voice sounded nervous. He sounded as if the Reverend *was* king of somewheres.

The front screen door banged softly, and Tunes padded over to where Kneebone stood quietly by.

'Sheriff stopped by the parsonage a few minutes ago, asking had I seen Mr Kneebone and Miss Tunes,' said the Reverend in a deep pulpit baritone. 'Said he wanted to ask some questions. I could've said I didn't know's I'd recognize them if I did see them.' He took a handkerchief from his pocket and wiped his face and neck. 'But I didn't,' he added slowly.

'Oh, dear Lord,' said Mazie, turning her eyes up. She pulled her apron up under her face and swayed to her other foot and back.

Jep pushed Tunes forward a step, but she shook loose from Jep's hand on her shoulder and moved right back to where Kneebone stood.

Kneebone broke the awkward silence by gesturing toward the front door, motioning them in out of the afternoon chill that settled over the woods as the sun lowered.

'Come in, Reverend, come in,' Jep said, as if the manners were his responsibility, and they all clumped up the front steps, right over my eavesdropping head. Chairs scraped and water hissed through the pipes beside me, glasses clinked, and I imagined Mazie and Tunes passing around glasses of water with ice from the little aluminium trays in the ancient refrigerator that slumped round-shouldered in the corner of the kitchen.

I could hear some of what was said, Jep doing most of the talking. It was mostly about me finding Jorge's body. Then the Reverend said in his well-tempered voice something about Sheriff, and me claiming Tunes was with me at the time.

There was a silence and then Jep asked Tunes a question, but I didn't hear an answer. Jep repeated the question, and again there was no reply. Then Jep exploded at her and there was a soft murmuring sound, as if they were trying to quiet him, and I heard the light pad of Tunes' feet as she ran up the stairs.

I looked back at Obie, afraid he'd bark or give us away somehow. He lay with his chin between his paws, one eye half-open and one ear twitching lazily. He cocked an eyebrow, but the eye fluttered shut again, as if weighted down by sleep.

They all lowered their voices; then a second set of feet went lightly up the stairs. Mazie and Tunes were in Tunes' second storey-bedroom, Their words floated out the window like the limp muslin curtains on a morning breeze.

'Don't mind Jep. He's just lookin' after your well-being,' Mazie said, clucking softly.

'He's got no business saying that . . .'

And I wondered what he'd said.

'I won't . . .'

'Now, now, chile,' Mazie said, in a soothing liquid voice. I couldn't hear anything distinctly after that.

Pretty soon everybody came out the front door again, and then it was the Reverend talking.

'I think there's not much doubt they're getting information from the boy that could be harmful to Miss Tunes,' the Reverend said. He measured his words carefully, like each was a dose from a spoon. 'I'll talk to Sheriff, make sure he knows the boy's not telling the truth.'

My blood boiled.

'I didn't lie!' I shouted. It came out involuntarily like an oath, as if I'd dropped an anvil on my foot.

There was a stunned silence as I hauled my cobwebby, dusty self out from under the stoop, bumping my head right smartly as I came.

'I'd advise you to keep her away from the boy,' the Reverend went on, like I hadn't appeared. 'Jep's right. Let her stay over there with him and his family for a while.'

The Reverend's head was shining bald down to within half an inch above his ears. A narrow fringe of long tight grey curls shook when he spoke. It looked for all the world like a seriously slipped halo.

'Buck, what you doing under there?' Kneebone asked, hands on his hips. 'What you sneakin' around for, crawling under there like a snake?'

'I came to tell you about what Sheriff said.' I dusted myself off. I was panting with emotion, and it sounded like I'd been running. 'I didn't tell him you were with me, Tunes. He already knew it.'

'How'd he know?' Tunes put her hands on her hips, just like Kneebone. But before I could answer, the Reverend interrupted.

'She's better off now with her own folks lookin' after her,' he said. He took a step closer to me so that his stomach nearly touched my chest. I didn't move. He had my dander up, and I wasn't about to let him have an inch.

'Next to Kneebone and Mazie, I'm close's she's got to her own folks,' I said, real quiet-like, my voice finally steadying. I couldn't match the Reverend's professional tone, but I had him hands down on sincerity.

Kneebone put one gnarly hand on my shoulder and the other on Tunes'.

'For now, Tunes'll stay home where she belongs,' Kneebone said to Jep.

Just then Obie came round the corner, trotted up to Tunes, and licked her hand, glad to see her. Then he sat, still sleepy, leaning against her leg. His tail swept up puffs of dust like a lazy broom. I didn't reckon anyone could have showed the Reverend any clearer who was family around there.

Chapter 6

Monday morning brought another big storm up the Bay, the sky growling and muttering for hours before first light. The cedars whipped and cracked outside my window, but the storm passed us by, leaving the air heavy, damp and unusually warm for April.

After breakfast I left early for the school bus so I could talk to Tunes alone. The day before, I'd told Kneebone and everybody all Sheriff had said, save the part about Jumbo claiming she and Jorge'd had a romance. I just couldn't bring myself to say it in front of Jep and Mazie and the Reverend. And Dad had his eye on me every second, so I couldn't get away again to talk to her. But I had to tell her.

She wasn't at the soybean field. I looked out the creek. Grey curtains of rain seemed to hang just at the mouth, and the breeze picked up as the storm passed on up to the next neck. It kept on that way all day, one storm after the other just marching up the Bay. But hardly any rain fell on the land.

In the distance I heard the rasp of Colonel Pickett's tractor starting up to plough in preparation for planting his soybean field. Kneebone ought to be out here ploughing our field, I thought.

Obie waited with me. A fox came skittering out of the hedge, two little pups behind her, golden fluff balls with bright buttons for noses. I stood still a couple of seconds to watch them, then flapped my arms to make them go back into the hedge where they'd be safe.

Just then Tunes came trotting up the track from her house, her braids bouncing up on end as she came. She wore her denim jumper, and I noticed her legs'd grown clear out from under it and it was tight in the armholes.

'You look like one of them silly sea gulls trying to take off,' she said, wrinkling her nose and showing her perfect teeth. I raised my hand and she slapped my palm.

She swung her backpack full of books off her shoulder and down to rest by her feet.

'Sheriff came last night,' she said.

'What'd he say?' I felt that lump of fear rise again in my gullet. She shrugged.

'He wanted to know what my relationship to Jorge was, and if I was with him Friday evening,' she said, scrunching up one corner of her mouth. 'I just told him we were all friends, that you and me were out dipping for bait Friday night. Thanks –'

'Tunes,' I broke in. 'Jumbo told Sheriff you and Jorge had some kind of romance going. Did he ask you?'

She shook her head then, as much as if trying to shake something out of it as simply saying no. And then she was silent for a bit.

'Sheriff said he wanted me to stay put,' she went on a few moments later, a smile playing at the corner of her mouth. 'So much for that old Reverend Toad telling me to go to Jep and Mazie's!'

Her bravery infected me, and in that moment the uneasy feeling I'd had – that things never would be right again – sailed right out of me like it had wings. I thought I must have put more weight on Jumbo's ability to turn Sheriff's suspicions on Tunes than was warranted. I scuffed my toes in the dirt to hide the rush of relief that swept over me.

'I was afraid you'd skip school,' I said then, just to change the subject.

As it turned out, it would have been a good thing if she had. I got more attention that Monday morning than I had in the whole time I'd been in school.

Tunes did what she normally did when folks got excited – pretended she didn't know me and made herself invisible. Of course, I lapped it up.

'Weren't you scared?' asked Mabe Tucker, the prettiest girl in the school. Her blue eyes looked deep into mine, admiration just written out plain across her sweet face. Her hulky boyfriend, Brooks Dowd, hovered, glaring, over her shoulder.

'What's to be scared of?' I asked. 'I didn't have anything to do with it, except finding him.'

The gossip about the murder of Jorge Rodrigues consumed Monday, and the day was over in a blur. I thought things would slow down and return to normal later in the week, but I was wrong.

It became generally known Sheriff had questioned Tunes, and of course she refused to say anything about it to anyone bold enough to ask. By Tuesday, talk around school had her a suspect, with whispers of charges about to be brought.

Several times I walked past a group of my classmates between classes and they fell silent. Several times I overheard somebody saying things about Tunes, like how 'odd' they thought she was, or how they'd seen how she was drawn to trouble. By midweek it had begun to wear on me.

'I always felt there was something . . . you know, *scary* about her,' I heard Laura Mae Alton, the most obvious teacher's pet in our class, whisper to her friend Willa Price as they walked behind me in the hall, their blonde heads pressed together. I whirled on them.

'You never had the sense to be scared,' I shouted.

Laura Mae looked stricken, and I continued to glare at her until she slunk away like a cur.

And the week slowed down to a crawl, each day harder to get through than the last.

But for Tunes and me after school, things seemed to have returned to remarkably near normal. And Dad had relaxed some at home. He did keep the key to the skiff, but at least he let me out of his sight, so Tunes and I could ride our bicycles through the late afternoon sunlight, skidding around corners in the sandy tracks that bordered the fields and setting up jumps with long boards from the loading ramps down at the packing shed.

Otherwise, Dad seemed preoccupied. He walked around the farm like he was continually in a hurry, like he did in midsummer, when things were most hectic. Tunes 'n' me could find plenty to do on land to keep us occupied, and we hardly missed the skiff.

Every once in a while dark thoughts flitted into my head and lurked there like ghosts. If Jumbo Rawlin had to hurt Tunes to save his own neck, sure as honeysuckle'd climb your leg he'd do it. Jorge was proof as positive as any!

There were distractions from those shivery thoughts.

When *The Eastern Shore News* came out Wednesday there was a picture of me and Sheriff, him asking me questions down at the dock. The paper quoted him saying I was near-professional, the way I was able to give information. They said it right there in the paper for Mabe Tucker and everybody to see.

There was nothing about Tunes, just that Sheriff was conducting an investigation.

Grades came out Thursday afternoon. That morning the principal of the middle school, Mr Warnock, came in during our homeroom period and called Tunes out to the office. She shifted her eyes downward, gathered her books, got up slowly from her desk, and walked straight and proud to where he stood waiting in the doorway.

The classroom fell dead silent. I was sure Sheriff'd come to take her away. My heart thundered in my chest. The same thought must've passed through everyone else's minds. As soon as Tunes' back disappeared into the dim hallway a few voices whispered. I glared over my shoulder in the direction of a snicker behind me, and silence returned.

As it happened, Tunes' term grades were straight A's, and she made the honour roll. I knew she'd hate that.

I didn't have any trouble avoiding the honours list, but Tunes made it in spite of herself. She was interested in just about everything and loved to read. But she did it out of interest, and not to get good grades. She hated attention and was afraid her getting good grades made the other black kids think she was uppity. Lots of the black kids didn't study for that very reason, so Tunes was the only black person in our class on the honour roll. Tunes would never tell me that, but many's the time I saw her eyes cast around to see there were plenty of grades as high as hers when test papers were handed back.

It wasn't that our school was so competitive. In fact, it wasn't at all. Mama had wanted me to go to the Broadwater Academy up the Bay a ways this year, because she thought I'd get a better education in a private school.

Mama was always correcting my grammar.

'You talk like some of your little classmates,' she said, making a prim mouth. She knew Dad and Gran would get angry with her if she said more, but I knew she meant I talked like Tunes, which I did a little. Tunes and I talked like the watermen, because that was who our friends were, who we wanted to be like.

There were no black kids at the Academy. It was supposed to have better teachers than the public schools. But Dad said he wasn't sure that was so. Besides, he said he wanted to support the public schools.

Anyways, one good thing about our farm falling on hard times was that we couldn't afford for me to go to the Academy.

I would have hated Mama driving me to school every day, passing by the soybean field, Tunes seeing me through the car window as she waited for the bus. And I'd have hated the long ride up the Bay with Mama asking me all kind of questions about homework and the 'nice' kids who went to the Academy, and who I couldn't care less about.

Some of them were come-heres, not Shore-born and -bred. Not more than a handful of them could fish worth a crow's squawk. They didn't have the same feeling for the land and the salt marshes and the deer and the foxes and the birds – all the things that made me and Tunes as much kin to the Bay as the cordgrass was to the sea meadows.

The come-heres were different, not peculiar and old-fashioned like Shore-bred kids. The come-heres dressed a little outlandish, like people in the malls across the Bay in Norfolk, with wedgy haircuts and baggy shorts that hung off their hips and down below their knees. With seventeen miles of Bay Bridge-Tunnel that cost half your life's savings to cross to the mainland and back, folks remained pretty isolated on the Eastern Shore.

None of the real Shore folks cared much either that they weren't up with the times. In fact it was a point of pride, made them feel somewhat superior.

That afternoon Obie waited for us as usual in the soybean field. He ran beside the school bus the last twenty yards or so before it got to our stop, and sat with his broad pink tongue lolling and dripping as we got off.

Instead of turning off down the lane toward home at the end of the track, Obie and I followed Tunes toward her house.

'Go on home, you,' she said. 'What you following me for?'

'I want to make sure you tell Kneebone you couldn't manage to stay off the honours list,' I said. 'I want to see the look on his face.'

Tunes let out a puff of air through her nose and unclenched her hand. In her palm the list was folded over eight times. She opened it and bent to flatten it out against her thigh.

'He'll be real proud,' I said. She turned without a word and continued on down the track, the unfurled paper in her hand. I was right: she most likely wouldn't have shown it to Kneebone if I hadn't followed her home. It wouldn't have been the first time I'd broken the same news to her father myself.

The hood of Kneebone's truck was propped up, and the sun shone mellow from its worn paint. I could see his bulgy-toed work boots underneath on the other side. He was bent over doing some work on the engine. The old hound came up to me, baying under her breath and prancing, trying to catch Obie's attention. Kneebone didn't so much as look up.

I threw a stick for the dogs to wrangle over. When Kneebone finally came out from under the hood, wiping his hands on a clean rag, he walked around the truck to where Tunes stood. She handed him the sweaty, creased yellow paper with the honours list typed on it. He read it, looked at Tunes, back to the paper, then at me, and back to Tunes.

Kneebone put one of his big old arms around each of us and hugged us up close to him. The knots of his elbows pressed into my back and I imagined how painful they must be. I buried my face in the line-dried smell of his shirt.

Everything will turn out right, I thought. It just had to.

When I got home, Mama was folding things away neatly in little plastic bags and placing them in a cardboard carton.

'What's to eat?' I asked, as I did when I first came home from school every afternoon. Gran sat me down at the bare wooden table with a corn muffin on a plate and a glass of milk.

Mama and Gran weren't talking, which wasn't unusual for them. Mama held up a pink-and-white checkered dress with a frilly lace collar.

'Think Tunes'll like this?' she asked.

'She never wore a ruffle in her life,' I said, eyeing the rows of tucks and lace on the front. Gran snorted behind me.

'Poor motherless child,' Mama said, as if we weren't even in the room with her, 'raised up by a man who wears steel-toed boots. Never had anyone to help her with things important to a girl.'

She tucked a matching pink-checked ribbon into a Baggie and placed it in the cardboard box atop the folded dress. She held up a pair of frilly underpants.

'She was top of the honour roll,' I said. Mama raised her eyebrows and smiled briefly.

'That's nice,' she said mildly, and I wondered whether she'd heard what I said.

'Mama, Tunes'll never wear that stuff!' I said, putting a spoonful of strawberry jam into a hole I'd made in my corn muffin. 'Where'd you get it?'

'They were going into the church rummage sale,' Mama said. 'She needs somebody to care about her, give her pretty things.'

'Tunes may need some things,' Gran said with gravity, 'but I dare say lace panties and ruffled dresses aren't among them!'

Mama pursed her lips. 'Why, whatever do you mean, Lillian?' she asked, looking over her shoulder at Gran.

'That girl needs heart kinds of things, and I don't mean lace-and-ruffle hearts,' said Gran. 'She needs someone to tell her she's smart, honest, a good person, things that'd ease her spirit, gentle her down some. Much as I love Kneebone, he sure isn't one to talk.'

Mama made a funny little click with her tongue, but said nothing. She and Gran had a lot of differences, and I suspected their practised silences saved them a lot of hard feelings.

That evening Obie and I sat down on the dock and watched the sun as it was about to set, waitin' for Gran to call us up for supper.

Worry returned to my stomach and lay there like a hard pile of beans. What if Jumbo caught up with Tunes? I was sure he was trying to pin what he'd done to Jorge on her, making up that story about a romance, and all. What if she wasn't charged and the attention turned toward him? If Tunes just disappeared under a cloud of suspicion everyone would assume she'd killed Jorge and then lit out somewheres. Sooner or later they'd stop looking for her and it'd be forgotten.

Jorge's misshapen head and grey knuckles and Miz Rawlin's swollen and bruised face and Kneebone's hound laying wet and dead on the shore kept appearing in my mind's eye, bringing on tears, and I had to fight like fury to keep them away.

As we sat there, the bald eagle that nested up the creek this last year came flying high over the water. He turned his head this way and that, looking for supper to take home. His wings fingered the wind; then he glided long and slow, passing lower over the water. He was a beautiful young bird that just about everybody in Northampton County knew well. He was small for an adult. But his feathers shone red and gold and he had those fierce proud eyes – almost like Tunes' eyes – that let you know there was no way he'd ever belong to anybody.

Last spring our neighbour Mrs Eastlake found him floundering in a ditch, sick near to death with insecticide poisoning. She called Fish and Wildlife and the rangers came and got him, banded him, and nursed him back to health.

The TV networks came to broadcast his release back into the wild a month later, and he became sort of a mascot for the wildlife protection people and the environmentalists.

The eagle showed up a few weeks later with his new mate to live upstream, near Post Creek Farm, where Mrs Eastlake lived, like he was going to look out for her from then on.

I watched him until he was clear out of sight, his wings moving with the ease of a creature with strength and energy to spare, and I envied him his freedom in the woods and over the creeks. His life was hard and filled with danger, but there was a simplicity to his daily search for food and taking up in his nest with his mate each evening.

Why couldn't Tunes and me hole up somewhere deep in the woods, with nothing but hunting and fishing to occupy us, where Sheriff and Mama and Dad would leave us be, where we'd be safe from Jumbo Rawlin? Obie sat beside me watching the eelgrass float down the creek on the outgoing tide, an occasional blue crab darting past. My hands and feet began to itch with wanting to do something to help Tunes, and not knowing for the life of me what.

Chapter 7

Tunes and I took up with the kinds of things we'd done before, so that we sometimes forgot for a whole afternoon at a time what'd happened to Jorge and the terrible suspicion that hung over Tunes. We heard nothing more of Sheriff's investigation.

We took up a project, which we did most years since we were little kids, to keep our minds off other things. The project was a target, a fine one of straw and canvas with a paper bull's-eye painted red in the centre. We thought it up in order to improve our marksmanship so's Kneebone and Dad would let us take our .22 rifles out to hunt rabbit. We were trying the target out with slingshots first.

One day after school Tunes and I went to the chicken shed at the edge of the field where we'd hidden our slingshots and a bag of chestnuts under a loose floor-board. Obie galloped ahead of us in a lop-eared, wagtailed streak of black fur.

We set off at a flat run, our feet shooshing through last year's carpet of damp brown leaves. Obie dashed off every few moments to check for fox and deer, but he'd come back soon enough and lope along beside us again, nose to the ground.

We dodged through the wood, past the sand track that ran along the side of the fields, back behind the ponds where the cattails waved, way out toward the farthest boundary of the farthest field.

The glade where our target was concealed was like a magical circle cleared by a large and kindly hand that had left just enough overhanging branches to protect us from the rain. And a small piece of sky opened overhead for checking the weather and the time. We didn't wear watches then – all we had to know about the time was when to go home, and most days the sun told us that.

Tunes got to the glade first and pulled aside the plastic tarpaulin. There was our target, damp but none the worse for the rain that had blown sideways across the Eastern Shore all week.

Obie snuffled in the bushes while Tunes took the first turn shooting. We shot with chestnuts because rocks were a rare commodity on the sandy spit that was the Eastern Shore. What stone there was had come over as ballast in the holds of British ships in colonial times, or, more recently, was trucked in to build roadbeds.

I stood near the target to keep Tunes informed of her accuracy. Each chestnut made a soft hissing sound before popping against the target, ever closer to the bull's-eye.

'That was only an inch off,' I said with reluctant enthusiasm. My admiration for her was boundless, but she was so much better than I was at most things I sometimes ended up discouraged.

I shifted my gaze back to see why the next chestnut hadn't whizzed into the bull's-eye. Tunes had set down her slingshot. She crept low, focused toward a clump of brush where Obie stood at attention, the end of his tail quivering with excitement.

A red flash of fur exploded out of the bush. A fox hesitated a moment, black nose working and eyes leaping to find her way to safety. Obie lunged forward almost at the same instant as the fox, but a Labrador retriever is no match in speed or grace for a scared fox, and she was gone, her tail out behind her like a flame.

I curled my tongue back behind my bottom teeth and gave a short, sharp whistle. Obie bounded back into the clearing. I looped my belt though his collar, and we continued on silently. Tunes dropped to her knees every few minutes to look at some sign the fox'd passed that way. The signs were invisible to me, but I was not surprised she was still on the fox's trail.

Tunes motioned us toward an ancient oak with branches that travelled low and far, in places just a foot or two from the ground. Obie and I climbed up into the third tier of branches and lay in a broad crotch to see where that fox'd got to. I was surprised at how far we'd come. The split-rail fence that marked the Timmons farm was just a few hundred feet away.

Tunes crept forward, wondrously silent even in her rubber fishing boots, her body crouched among the scrub, which wore garlands of bittersweet vine.

Suddenly a riot of squawking and screeching and shouting and yapping burst from the Timmons farmyard. Tunes stood, arms out at her sides, on her tiptoes to see. The fox bolted through the brush, a heavy white hen clamped in her mouth. One wing flapped weakly. A few seconds later three large grey hound dogs burst into the clearing, gaining on the fox.

'You worthless hounds!' a hoarse voice shouted from behind the barn. 'Git back here!' It was Emmett Timmons, the bad-tempered man who owned the chicken farm. His wife was Tunes' and my English teacher. I saw him then, in a dirty red-plaid jacket, thrashing at the thick brush at the edge of the barnyard. The dogs continued on after the fox, which dodged through the brush well ahead of them.

'You curs! Pick on somebody your own size,' Tunes shouted, hurling a stout stick after them. The dogs slunk back. It was just enough time for the fox to head for thicker brush, where she'd increase her advantage and make good her escape with the hen.

'Stop, you damn thief!' Emmett Timmons squinted through the brush. He whistled for the pack, but they paid him no mind. He waded into the thicket, flailing at low-hanging branches and cussing. And then he caught sight of Tunes, chucking another stick after his hounds. They scattered, heads and tails down.

'You worthless sunsabitches!' he shouted after his dogs. 'Get that nigger!' His voice splintered with fury.

'Run, Tunes!' I shouted. But she stood still like she'd taken root there. Obie gave a fearsome low growl. I clamped my hand around his muzzle. 'Hush up!' I hissed in his ear.

'Stop!' Emmett Timmons shouted, his voice high-pitched and crackled. 'Come back here, you chicken thief!' He thrashed into the brush, his large pink stomach peeping out from the bottom of the jacket as he flailed his arms.

With an almost casual glance over her shoulder, Tunes turned and trotted away. The dogs, as if taking courage from Emmett Timmons, regrouped and loped after her, gathering speed after a few seconds. By then I was frozen with fear up in my tree.

But Tunes was quick as she was silent, and within seconds there wasn't a sign of her. The dogs bayed after her, then circled, and I couldn't tell whether they'd caught her scent or had picked up the fox's trail again.

Emmett Timmons waded around through the thick brush at the edge of the farm, still cussing and kicking at the underbrush. I clamped my arm tight around Obie's neck and leaned my cheek against the giant limb that held us.

The dogs still barked, their excited yaps thinned and fractured by the half mile of trees between them and where I lay with Obie. After a piece there was no further sound from the Timmons farmyard. I reckoned it was safe to get down. I took my belt from Obie's collar and set him loose with his nose to the ground.

'Tunes!' I called softly, my voice shaking. A boot dangled down from a branch in a thick old dogwood, as if testing water. Then she dropped, knees bent to catch the shock of the four-foot fall. I wondered how she'd got up that high. She didn't look at us. It was as if she didn't know we were there.

In a near crouch she darted among the trees and thick hanging vines, silent and quick as a thrush in the darkening wood, Obie and me trailing behind. The rain had slowed to a faint drizzle. Our breath puffed out in white wispy clouds and dissipated quickly around our heads as we ran.

'What about the target?' I asked, puffing. She shrugged.

'Better get on home,' she said.

I had an uneasy feeling that the target – which we'd schemed over to pass the time since Jorge's death – was no longer important to her. Projects had played a large part in our friendship up until then, and I'd grown wary of change.

The spring before, it had been turtle crossings on the county roads. Every spring thousands of box turtles lumbered from the brackish ponds to the creeks or from one pond to another and back again. And every year thousands of them lay dead, their shells cracked in half on the roadbeds, the crows making off with their innards.

Tunes and I marked the crossings with signs that said SLOW DOWN! TURTLE CROSSING. In the spots where people tended not to slow down, we put logs across the road so they had to stop and kick the logs over into the ditches. Neither of us would ever have abandoned that project.

I didn't like the way Tunes'd waved off the target as though it was childish, like I was silly for taking it so seriously.

We headed toward the shed to restash our slingshots.

'Maybe old Emmett Timmons didn't see us after all,' I said, enticing her to refocus on our project. 'Maybe he was just siccing his dogs on that fox . . .'

A sudden swish in the brush startled us, and we both went up on the balls of our feet, hearts in our throats. A hoof struck the spongy moss floor of the wood, and Tunes laughed as a tawny flank flashed among the laurels. It was the old whitetail doe who'd been hanging around for the potato peelings Kneebone put out each evening in the clearing behind the house.

Tunes' pace settled into a jog, with Obie and me tagging behind her. We heard the steady *thunk* of Kneebone chopping wood long before we broke into the clearing behind the house.

Kneebone straightened painfully and leaned on the handle of the axe. He pushed up the brim of his old felt hat, and the veins in his forehead stood out like ropes. He look fragile, despite the bulging of his arm muscles where his red flannel shirtsleeves were rolled back.

'You ought've left that for me,' Tunes said.

'No tellin' where you been and when you'd be back.'

He said it with neither rancour nor humour, and handed the axe over to her.

Tunes removed her oilskin slicker and bent to retrieve another log from the woodpile. Kneebone went up the back steps. While he started the fire for supper, Tunes lent the full strength of her broad shoulders and back to the axe.

'Well,' I said. 'I'd best be going.' It was getting on for six o'clock, and I daren't be late for supper.

'See you.' Tunes grinned up at me and heaved her shoulders into another mighty swing. Her smile reassured me things were still all right. I was just turning toward the track for home when Kneebone's old hound dog dragged herself out from under the front stoop, and sniffed the air. She set to baying, and Tunes stopped chopping for a second, wiped her brow.

'Hush up!' she said, but the old hound stood with her feet splayed and her head back, her voice hissy as an old goose. Kneebone came out onto the front stoop. An old white farm truck bumped over the dirt track toward us. The sight of it set my heart to hammering again.

The truck stopped a dozen yards from where Tunes stood leaning against the axe handle, me next to her. Emmett Timmons got out, adjusted his cap over his close-cropped reddish hair, and walked toward us.

'Evenin', Mr Timmons,' said Kneebone. But Emmett Timmons said nothing.

He walked slow and deliberate toward Tunes and me until he loomed large and wide before us. Emmett Timmons stuck an enormous forefinger into Tunes' face, the nail completely outlined in black grime, just inches from her nose.

'I'm awarnin' you,' he said. His voice was a low growl. Kneebone stepped stiffly down from the stoop.

'You steal another chicken and I'll beat you so's you can't walk,' Emmett Timmons said, jabbing his finger closer with each word, the final stab hitting the end of her nose. Tunes blinked. The farmer turned to me then and glared, his eyebrows low over deepset eyes. But he said nothing further.

Kneebone moved into the narrow space between Emmett Timmons and Tunes. She blinked again and swallowed hard.

'No cause to menace this chile,' Kneebone said, his voice quiet. 'She don't steal. You can come in an' see. There's no chicken here.'

Emmett Timmons did not back away. 'I seen her,' he said. 'And him,' he added, swinging his pointing finger toward me.

'Tunes?' Kneebone said. 'Buck?' He inclined his head over his shoulder toward Tunes and me, but kept his eyes on Emmett Timmons.

'Buck and me was tracking a red fox in the wood over near the Timmons farm,' Tunes said, her voice steady. ''Fore I knew it, that little vixen came streaking by, one of those white leghorn hens clamped in her mouth. Next thing I knew, three big old dogs came bursting out after her.'

'Didn't I tell you about staying away from the Timmons farm?' Kneebone said, turning to look at her.

'Yessir,' she said. Tunes looked her father in the eye. 'We were so fixed on that little fox we didn't see we'd got so close. We turned tail and ran, and the dogs kept on after the fox.'

Kneebone turned back toward Emmett Timmons. 'Tunes say a fox stole your chicken, then it was a fox stole your chicken.'

Emmett Timmons narrowed his eyes and leaned closer to Kneebone and Tunes, and me beside them. But we all stood our ground.

'You think you can get away with this? We'll see. I'll have Sheriff call on you. Least he'll know what's going down, these parts. Don't think he's forgot about you.'

My heart near stopped at the mention of Sheriff, which brought back for the first time that afternoon the other worse trouble Tunes was in.

'Sheriff's welcome here,' Kneebone said calmly. 'He won't find no chicken neither. Now I'll thank you to get off my propity.'

When Emmett Timmons'd gone, spinning his wheels and fishtailing his truck all over the sandy track, Kneebone climbed the back steps again and turned from the stoop to watch the taillights until they had disappeared. He went in to make his cornbread without a word. Tunes let her breath out all at once.

'Your mama's going to wonder where you are,' she said.

'See you in the morning,' I answered. My mouth felt dry and papery. Tunes went back to her chopping.

Chapter 8

Next morning the wind turned colder, and rain slid down it sidewise. I sat at the breakfast table with Mama and Gran. Dad was out doing farm chores, which he was hard at before first light every morning. I bolted my eggs and toast, while Obie lay under the table, waiting with hope in his every heartbeat for something to drop.

'Can I be excused?' I asked when my plate was empty.

'Ask properly,' Mama said.

'May I be excused, please?'

She came around the table and took my chin in her hand, inspecting my face for egg and my hair for unruly tufts of red that had shaken loose from water-slicked comb tracks.

'Land, child!' she said. 'It looks as if you've been at your head with an eggbeater.'

As always, Gran stood up for me: 'Messy hair doesn't matter,' she said, 'long's what's inside is straight.' It was a basic difference between the two of them that Gran didn't hold much with the appearance of things.

I pulled my slicker on over my head, and Gran handed me my sou'wester at the back door. She yanked me back as I darted past.

'Put it on,' she said, meaning business as always. I tied the sou'wester under my chin and ran to the edge of the soybean field beside the wood to meet Tunes and wait with her for the school bus.

I got there before her, so I chucked sticks into the field for Obie, who ran back and forth, building me a pile of kindling.

'Hey!' I shouted when I saw Tunes running across the end of the field. I stood with my hands by my sides, and rain dripped off my sleeves. Tunes' yellow slicker looked almost neon against the blue-grey mist of rain. I turned up the brim of my sou'wester, happy to have it then, and the rain drizzled down the back of it.

Tunes dropped her backpack to the ground.

'Hey yerself,' she said, pausing just a second to catch her breath. She squinted her eyes and her voice was higher than usual, and I knew she had a story to tell. Tunes acted out stories more'n told them.

'Sheriff came calling again last night,' she said, 'just like Emmett Timmons said.'

I swallowed hard.

'Did he say anything about the investigation?' Tunes shook her head.

'Not directly,' she replied. 'But he wanted me to know he hasn't forgotten. Kneebone and me were just finishing up the dishes. He came in, looking around like he expected to find that old white hen still flapping in a corner.'

Emmett Timmons told Sheriff his chickens had been disappearing and that he'd seen Tunes out in the woods behind his barn. Sheriff wanted to hear what she had to say. As she told me, Tunes' eyes were fierce and golden like an osprey's eyes when she's protecting her nest out on one of the marker pilings in the middle of the creek.

'I really didn't feel like telling him, you know?' she said. She stared at me a moment, her gaze relentless. I nodded. 'I wanted to remind him that me and Kneebone are the black family lives closest to the Timmons farm. Every time something goes missing or broken there, the Timmonses always let it be known they think we're responsible.'

She looked down toward Pungotuck Creek, which meandered among swaying islands of yellow cordgrass to where the Bay glistened in sun that shone beyond the storm.

'Why didn't he come looking at your house for that chicken?' she asked. I had no answer for her, and so she went on with her story.

'But I told him what happened, everything except for Emmett Timmons siccing his hounds on us. Sheriff looked around the room several times. You could smell the fried ham from supper. Wasn't a chicken feather in sight.

'Still, he went over to the 'frigerator and swung open the door. There were eggs, apples, leftover ham, and a pitcher of grape juice. But no chicken.

'Then he looked in the plastic garbage bin, pulled out the bundle of garbage Kneebone'd wrapped up in newspaper, and opened it on the drainboard. Inside was coffee grounds and greasy paper from the ham, and a few pieces of bone that were too sharp to give to the hound.

'Then we all went outside with Kneebone's flashlight. Kneebone led the way. He wanted to be sure Sheriff saw all there was to see. Took him to the mulch pile. No feathers there, no chicken bones. Then to the oil drum where Kneebone burns the trash. Sheriff got a stick and stirred through the ashes, then went back to the mulch pile and lifted up layer after layer. No feathers, no chicken bones. He even looked in the hound's dish.

'Then Sheriff went to his car and got out a stronger flashlight and looked over everything again.

'I was standing up on the stoop. When Sheriff was done, he came over and said to me, "You best stay away from the Timmons farm, Tunes. I told you to stay put, remember?" And Kneebone told him, "Smith propity goes clear up to the Timmons barnyard. She wasn't trespassin".'

'Then Sheriff, he goes, "You're already in enough trouble," and tips his hat and leaves.' Tunes still had that gimlet-eyed look that always put up a wall between us and left me feeling itchy.

'I know just what Sheriff was thinking. I'm surprised he didn't come to your house just to warn your daddy to keep you away from that bad nigger girl that steals chickens and maybe a lot worse.' I winced at her words.

'It was at least as much my fault as yours,' I said somewhat lamely. She waved her hand, dismissing me impatiently. I knew she didn't like to bully me. And I couldn't blame her for resenting Sheriff's not coming to see if I had taken that chicken, or his not thinking I might've played a bigger part in Jorge's death.

She said nothing for a few moments. Obie kept bringing sticks over for Tunes to throw until he'd moved near half the pile over in front of her feet. She didn't seem to see him.

Then the school bus lumbered into view. I wanted to tell her I thought it unfair, and that Mama and Dad and Gran didn't think she'd killed Jorge. But I stood there miserable and mute. When the school bus had turned around at the end of the field, come back up, and stopped for us, we got on and went our separate ways.

I sat with a freckle-faced kid named Dewey Morgan, who folks sometimes said looked just like me. Tunes walked right past us and sat alone on the other side of the aisle as if she didn't know me, which wasn't so unusual.

Our lifelong friendship ended when we got on the school bus each morning, not to resume until the bus'd disappeared down the county road after leaving us off each afternoon. Once we reached the old wood school building down in Skunk Hollow, there were a few guys I shot hoops with at recess and lunchtime.

But Tunes was mostly by herself. She pretended she didn't care about anybody, but I knew she did. Even if she was a loner, she wanted people to like her, respect her at least.

Obie trotted down the road after the bus a bit. Soon he turned into the soybean field and headed back toward the farm, nose down, thinking what adventure he might busy himself with until we returned.

Dewey and I talked about something, I don't remember what. I was still very agitated about Sheriff's visit. I was also worried it would refocus Sheriff's attention on Tunes as a suspect in Jorge's killing. And our unfinished conversation about why she was a suspect and I wasn't in both cases ate at me.

Black folks and white folks in Northampton County hadn't changed as much in their dealing with each other as they had in places where time moved faster, like across the Bay in Norfolk. Everybody here knew pretty much where they stood in relation to everybody else. The black people who had jobs worked mainly for white people and called them ma'am and sir. And white folks expected it to be that way. Even those who considered themselves broad-minded didn't ever quite cross the lines.

My family was different, or at least I always thought they were. The white Smiths had relied on the black Smiths all the way back to the 1700s, when our family came over from England and settled this farm, and the black Smiths came from Africa as slaves. My family had laboured right beside them clearing the land and working it all down the years. Once the slaves were freed, they took our family name, Smith, and stayed on.

Mama and Dad loved Tunes and Kneebone, and it was more than overflowing Christian charity. They valued the black Smiths like family, as had my granddaddy, and his granddaddy, and his before them. But it soon became evident Mama and Dad's love had faltered.

I can see now that none of us Smiths, black or white, had ever lost sight of that line of otherness, and it came to divide us more bitterly than if the love had never been there at all.

Growing up where we did, Tunes and I had both teethed on racism. And yet we were blind to colour, each as far's the other was concerned, and we thought of people in terms of 'otherness', according to whether they cared as much as we did about the Bay and creeks and woods and all of the creatures in them.

All day I felt the weight of that unfinished conversation. I kept hoping she'd say something – or make some sign to dispel the last words between us – but she didn't.

Then the class just before lunch, which was English, Miz Timmons came into the room with a sour look on her face. My heart sank. In front of me, Tunes' spine was straight and tense.

The week before, Miz Timmons had surprised us with a test. It was on Henry James's *The Turn of the Screw*, which Tunes and I had read together. I hated it. Tunes thought it was wonderful, and had explained it to me. Miz Timmons called on Laura Mae, her favourite student, to hand back the tests.

When we had our papers, Miz Timmons stood before the class and spoke real low, like she was doing a slow burn.

'What would you say if I told you a student had cheated on last week's test?' she asked. Nobody answered. 'Laura Mae?' Laura Mae, who didn't seem the least abashed at being Miz Timmons's pet, stood up beside her seat and answered.

'I think that person should not only flunk the test but flunk the entire course.' Laura Mae looked about her for approval, her blonde ponytail swinging out around her head.

'Yes!' said Miz Timmons, whose face had coloured to the shade of a red delicious apple. 'That's just what I think, too!'

Tunes sat still as a stone in front of me. I looked over her shoulder. Miz Timmons had scrawled across the top of her test paper in angry red letters: 'I don't believe you wrote this. It looks to me as if it was copied.' She had circled the big red F that she had drawn across the entire page so everyone could see it.

'And what do you have to say, Miss Smith?' Miz Timmons asked, standing before Tunes, her feet apart and her arms folded across her chest.

'Nothing,' Tunes said under her breath.

'Speak up!' said Miz Timmons. 'I asked you a question.'

Tunes' head came up and she said out loud, 'I have nothing to say.' It was all I could do to keep myself from shouting that Tunes hadn't cheated. But I knew she'd never forgive me if I did.

Miz Timmons scolded for five minutes, packing back and forth in front of the class, her green-checkered skirt swirling out around her as she turned.

'You kids are given the chance for a good education, just like all the other kids. All you're interested in is trouble,' Miz Timmons said. 'Sometimes I think . . .'

She looked like she had a bad taste in her mouth, but she reconsidered saying what she sometimes thought. She just pressed her lips into a thin line and turned her back.

'. . . waste of taxpayers' money,' she muttered as she walked back to her desk.

Tunes didn't say a word, but it took all of my will not to say anything. My ears burned and tears pricked at the back of my eyes. When we got off the school bus that afternoon my voice came out high-pitched and loud.

'You're the smartest kid in our class,' I said, flapping my hands at her. She didn't answer, just kept stalking ahead of me, across the edge of the soybean field, down into the piney wood.

'She had no right to accuse you of cheating,' I said, getting in front of her. But she wouldn't stop, and I had to walk backward fast to stay in her face. 'You should have stood up to her.' She kept right on, and I was out of breath.

'You weren't afraid to stand up to Emmett Timmons when he sicced his dogs on you. Why're you afraid of her?'

Tunes kept trudging, refusing to be provoked. She headed off the main path and let a branch go so that it swished at my face. I kept on after her.

'She had no right to fail you . . . Anyway, how could you copy, right there in the classroom with her and everybody watching?'

Tunes whirled to face me then, arms rigid at her sides, and her eyes were furious.

'What d'you know?' she demanded. 'Reason she accused me of cheating is she thinks I stole her chickens. She can't prove it 'cuz I didn't do it. She's just mad she couldn't get the best of Kneebone and me.'

'You got to stand up to her, Tunes, not let her get away with it!' I was beside myself with frustration and anger.

Tunes didn't want to talk. She turned her back and headed off toward the creek. But I wasn't near ready to let go of it. Tunes went on down to the creek, and I ran through the woods, down the track to the packing shed, where I found Kneebone at work on an irrigation pump.

'Kneebone,' I said, fighting for breath, 'Tunes got an F on her English test. Miz Timmons accused her of cheating, and I know Tunes didn't cheat.'

With deliberation Kneebone tightened a fitting before he looked at me, and suddenly I felt foolish, the way I'd run through the wood like the Devil himself was at my back, and acted like a ninny, all scared and sissified.

'Why you telling me this, Buck?'

''Cause it isn't fair and I can't stand up to Miz Timmons myself. A grownup has to.'

'And what do you think that will accomplish?' He stood and pushed the cap back off his forehead with his gnarled hand. 'You think if I go in and talk to her she'll change Tunes' grade?'

'You can't let someone accuse her of cheating,' I said. 'At least set the record straight.'

Kneebone looked at me a long time.

'*Your* daddy could march right in there and Miz Timmons'd listen to him,' he said. 'And she might even change your grade. You know and I know and Tunes know she couldn't fail a test if she tried. But if I go in there, Miz Timmons'd only make things harder for Tunes.'

'You won't know if you don't try,' I said. I was near tears then, and I knew arguing with Kneebone would be a thankless job. I turned and ran out of the packing shed and didn't stop until I got to the end of our driveway.

That evening after supper, Mama and Gran cleared the dishes and set to making bread. The smell of yeast and crust wafted from room to room, and I wondered what was on Mama's mind.

I went into Dad's study, where he sat at his desk in a hot white pool of light from the lamp. Little twinkles danced from the wire rims of his glasses. I stood before his desk a moment, hesitant to interrupt him. Finally he looked up. 'Yes, son?'

I asked if I could talk to him and he told me to sit down. He put his pen down and took off his glasses. I told him about Emmett Timmons and the chicken. When I'd finished, Dad did what I'd expected, and asked why I hadn't told him last night.

'Well, because I didn't think it mattered,' I said, knowing I wouldn't get away that simply. 'Until now, that is,' I said. Then I rushed on before Dad could interrupt to tell what'd happened with Tunes in English class and what Kneebone'd said.

'Do you think,' I asked when I'd finished, 'do you think you could talk to Miz Timmons?' Dad took a long, deep breath and rubbed his eyes with both hands.

'Tunes,' he said. 'How can one little girl get into so much trouble?'

'It's not fair,' I said, feeling like the whole issue of Tunes and trouble was wildly out of control. 'She didn't steal chickens, and she had nothing to do with Jorge's death. And she didn't cheat on her test.'

'Don't you think that the question of Tunes' cheating is up to Kneebone and Tunes to look after?' he asked.

'Kneebone says Miz Timmons wouldn't listen to him,' I said, 'but she'd listen to you. We can't just let it go, with everybody thinking Tunes cheated! So many things're against her, and she didn't do anything to hurt anybody.'

'It may not be fair, Buck,' he said. 'But Kneebone and Tunes've got to get themselves straight with the Timmonses, and with Sheriff. And you have to stay out of it. Fairness isn't the issue here.'

'But, Dad, if – '

'It's time you finished your homework and got to bed.'

'Dad – '

'Get on with you,' he said, putting his glasses back on his face, hooking the wire rims behind his ears. I sat there a second thinking about trying harder to persuade him, but he looked up as he reached for his pen and I knew there wasn't any use.

'Night,' I said.

'Good night, son,' he said, and added when I was almost in the doorway, 'You got to learn, Buck, you can't do something about everything that seems unfair.' I kept walking. 'Hear me?'

'Yessir,' I said.

'Good night,' he said, already back at his papers.

'Night.'

I went up to my room and sat at my desk, but I'd already done my math. Then I slipped down the back stairs and out the kitchen door for one last walk down to the dock with Obie before bed.

Next morning Tunes wasn't at the soybean field. Kneebone took her to school in his pickup truck. I saw them pull up during homeroom period, and on the pretext of going to the lavatory, I walked down the hall toward the parent-teacher conference room beside the principal's office a few moments later. I passed Tunes alone in the hall, headed toward class. She locked eyes with me, but kept walking, her backpack slung over one shoulder. I stopped and called out to her, but she kept walking away from me in the direction I'd just come from.

I walked slowly past the conference room. Kneebone stood before the table where Miz Timmons sat, looking up from under her eyebrows and shaking her finger at him. His big, calloused hands hung awkwardly at his sides and his nut-brown head was bent as he listened to her. He looked like a big kid being scolded.

I walked back to class with a heavy heart. I hated seeing Kneebone humbled like that. I was angry with Kneebone for not fighting back, and at Miz Timmons for treating him like a child. Suddenly I grasped what Dad had been trying to tell me about staying out of things that seemed unfair. I was sorry I'd ever told Kneebone about the cheating accusation.

The image of Tunes that afternoon – eyes full of scorn, hands rigid at her sides, yelling at me, thinking I was a righteous fool – kept coming back to me for a long time after. She didn't speak to me for a week. And there was another lesson I never forgot: when it came to right and wrong, things that made sense for me and my family were different for Tunes and Kneebone and other black folks.

Chapter 9

Things picked up on the farm. If there was progress in the investigation into Jorge's death, we heard nothing about it. While I was desperate for information, I was terrified that what I'd learn was that Jumbo'd done other things to implicate Tunes further. That curious state of limbo began to feel oddly familiar, almost normal.

Kneebone was busy ploughing and laying irrigation lines. The itinerant labourers moved into the camps down the road and began planting cucumbers and squash in our fields. Bending over flats of seedlings in their bright-coloured shirts and straw hats, they looked like rows of flowers bobbing over the furrows.

Dad really was busy then, as the planting got under way. Every afternoon he'd wheel into the driveway in a cloud of dust, take off his hat outside the kitchen door, and slap it against his trousers to shake off the loose dirt before coming in for dinner.

Gran always fussed at him because he lost so much weight. It was hard to see how that was possible. Every noonday during planting, and all through summer and the harvest, Gran cooked up a roast or a chicken, ham biscuits, cabbage, iced tea, and a pie or cake or both. It looked like enough to feed an army, and Dad and Kneebone, Mama, Gran, and Tunes and me on week-ends, we'd pretty near clean it up.

Even so, by midsummer Dad's work trousers'd be sagging around his hips. And Gran said he was like to embarrass everybody by dropping them when he least expected it.

Kneebone came and went several times a day, starting in our kitchen with a steaming cup of coffee before first light each morning.

Mama took her turn working the farm machinery, plus her work with Gran in the house and garden, plus the farm payroll for the season.

It was about then that not being able to go out on the creek began to wear on me. Tunes and I spent some time fishing and crabbing off the end of our dock. And we both became dead aims with our slingshots.

We each had more chores than we'd had during winter. Mine were about equally divided between the farm and helping Mama and Gran in the house and garden, some of it that seemed more busy work than my usual chores. But I did everything without complaining.

Tunes often helped Kneebone around the farm weekends and sometimes baby-sat Mazie's grandbabies after school and evenings.

Mama liked to invite me to keep her company when she ran errands. She let me drive out over the farm tracks. When we got to the county blacktop roads, I climbed out and got in the passenger side while Mama slipped behind the wheel.

'You drive well,' Mama said to me one Saturday afternoon. We'd brought the truck, and Obie rode in the bed. 'Nice and smooth, without turning the wheel too much.'

She was just making talk. Nobody could drive smooth on the series of unpaved tracks that led around the fields and from the farm to the county road. Dad had to grade the main oystershell drive every two months or so, and still the grey-white stuff piled up a week later into little washboard ridges that'd like to make your teeth chatter clear out of your head. And every time it rained, ruts formed in the sand tracks.

I didn't feel much like talking, and Mama seemed happy to natter on about the garden. We were on our way to pick up some plants for the perennial border that Mama'd ordered over to the Northampton Cooperative, just up Route 13 a few miles.

I loaded the flats of seedlings into the truck bed while Mama talked to Mrs Parson about the weather. Mrs Parson's husband, Tad, was a clerk in Sheriff's office.

I made several trips with the plants, then came back for a sack of bone meal and a couple of bales of peat.

'Tad says they're about to arrest the coloured girl,' said Mrs Parson, and I froze in my tracks. 'Someone found the gun killed that Mexican in the creek where they found the body and turned it over to Sheriff. It was hers. Didn't I hear that girl was in trouble over at the Timmonses?'

Mama nodded. That simple little inclination of Mama's head at the news Tunes might be arrested seemed to me the worst ever act of treachery. Mama was about to speak, but something made her look over her shoulder, and when she saw me poised in mid-stride, still halfway across the floor from the loading dock, my hands suspended at my sides, she clamped her mouth shut.

I turned blindly and ran for the door. 'Buck!' she called out after me.

And then, as if I hadn't already had more than I could deal with, I bumped bang into Jumbo Rawlin, who'd just come in through the doorway. Banging into Jumbo Rawlin was something like colliding with a tree at a dead run. I bounced clear off him and stood back, my heart pounding and quivering inside my chest.

He looked at me for a brief second, then tipped his hat toward Mama and Mrs Parson.

'Morning, ladies,' he said pleasantly. 'Jen, Miz Parson.'

'Morning, Mr Rawlin,' Mama said. She smiled at him and signed for the seedlings.

I turned, wheeled through the door, and made for the cab of the truck.

Every nerve in my body felt raw. I wondered if Miz Parson really knew Sheriff was going to arrest Tunes. And I just didn't understand how people could turn a blind eye to everything Jumbo'd done. It seemed all Northampton County – including my mother – bowed down at his feet. Bitterness and fear seethed inside me.

Mama came out just a second later, but stopped, turned in the doorway, and said something I couldn't hear. She still wore a faint smile, the same kind of smile she bestowed on the minister after church every Sunday, as she climbed into the truck cab.

I turned and watched her back up, then manoeuvre out onto the highway.

'Mama, how could you?' I asked.

'What, dear?' she asked in her mild and maddening way. She looked into the rearview mirror.

'How could you let Mrs Parson talk that way about Tunes?'

'Why, honey, you just have to face up to it. Tunes is in real trouble – '

'And how could you smile at Mr Rawlin? This is his fault! Tunes didn't do nothing.'

'*Anything*, dear. *Any*thing, not nothing.' She laid her hand over my fist, clenched beside her on the seat. 'I know you're upset, Buck, but you have to face up to it. Tunes is in real trouble, and I doubt it's because she didn't do anything. As for Mr Rawlin – well, there's no need to be uncivil . . .'

I snatched my hand out from under hers and flung myself into the farthest corner of the front seat. I looked out the window, all atwitch with nervous energy. As angry and frightened as I was, I felt as if pure adrenaline pumped through my veins. I had to get to Tunes right quick. That was the only thing I could do.

When we got home, Sheriff's white wagon stood in the driveway, lights whirling and blinking, doors open. Kneebone was in the back seat. My heart beat so fast I could scarce breathe. At least Sheriff hadn't caught up with Tunes yet.

Gran stood in the doorway, drying her hands on a white dish towel. She walked slowly down the front steps, listening to Sheriff, the sun shining through her thick white hair. She looked up as we pulled into the driveway.

Sheriff came over to the open window where I sat on the passenger's side before Mama even stopped the truck.

'Buck, do you know where Tunes is?' he asked, leaning in. I shook my head. 'I want the truth now,' he said, cocking his head to show he meant business. Obie jumped out over the side of the truck bed. He pranced around Sheriff excitedly, sensing the tension in his voice.

'No, sir,' I said. 'Unless she's around the farm.'

'Her father says he hasn't seen her since yesterday.'

Sheriff nodded his head toward where Kneebone sat in the back seat of his wagon. 'I figured if anybody'd know where she was, you would.'

I did know Tunes was over at Mazie's, where she baby-sat some Saturday afternoons. But I wasn't about to tell Sheriff that. I looked at Kneebone. He returned my look quietly.

'Buck hasn't left the farm, except with Senior or me,' Mama said, ducking low to see Sheriff's face through the passenger window. 'We haven't seen hide nor hair of Tunes the last two days.'

Sheriff doffed his hat and turned on his heel without a fare-thee-well.

'Sheriff!' Mama called after him, and he turned his head as she scrambled down from the cab. 'If Kneebone says he hasn't seen Tunes since last night, that's when he last saw her.'

Sheriff all but ran the rest of the way to his wagon, put it into reverse, and made two small ruts in the lawn and clipped the rhododendron hedge as he cut back out the driveway, ignoring the neat circular oystershell turn-around.

'I never!' Gran said.

'Is he going to arrest her?' asked Mama.

'Well, he didn't rightly say,' said Gran, still looking after the swirl of coloured lights and the puff of grey dust that followed Sheriff off the farm.

But I knew what Sheriff was up to. It was what I'd been dreading and fearing all along: that Sheriff'd found some critical piece of evidence and come to take Tunes away. Tunes' gun surely was a critical piece of evidence.

I picked up a flat of seedlings and carried it out to the perennial border, the skin prickling across my shoulders as I walked around to the back of the house. Instead of returning for the rest of the plants, I dropped the flat in the shade beside the border and ran to the shed, where my bicycle lay against a bale of burlap.

I moved so quickly even Obie hadn't seen me, and I was glad, because I didn't want him following me down the track and across the country road the back way over to Mazie's house.

I wasn't quite sure what I'd do if Jep was home, because he wasn't likely to do what Mazie'd do: invite me in for homemade bread or a cookie. Not that I had time or appetite for a cookie that day.

I turned my bicycle into the narrow quarter-mile dirt track, and bumped over sandy ruts down to the glade where the big old house hunched among the oak trees.

It was a dilapidated three-storey structure with weathered grey clapboard siding. Mazie and Jep had five children, and they moved in and out with such frequency you couldn't tell who might be living there at any given time.

Two of the older girls had little ones who stayed with their grandma all the time. One of the girls went to high school days and worked at the azalea nursery afternoons and evenings. The other daughter was a day-shift receptionist over at the hospital.

Mazie also had a niece staying with her, and her husband and their baby, and Jep's nephew. It was a houseful but there seemed no end of beds, and they made a place for anyone who wanted to stay under the sagging roof, behind the cracked windowpanes, passing in and out through the door so regularly nobody ever bothered to close it.

Mazie always had a pot of soup on the stove and a batch of cornbread or biscuits in the oven and a gallon jar of sun tea on the back step waiting for sugar.

I had to get off and walk the bike quickly the last bit of the driveway, which wound among the largest of the trees. Tunes' little cousin DanDan stood in the shade near the corner of the house in a pair of overalls, hugging a short length of plastic pipe to his chest. Jep's hound dog came baying hoarsely out from under the house.

I ran straight past them, dropping my bike against the big old oak at the nearest edge of the yard, and took the three steps up onto the front stoop in one leap.

'Mazie! Tunes! Anybody home?' I was clear out of breath.

DanDan moved into the middle of the driveway, watching me with his enormous round eyes.

'Hi, DanDan!' I said. I leapt off the stoop and bent to the level of the little boy's face. 'Where's Tunes and Grandma Mazie?'

He said nothing, looking into my face solemnly. He put a fat forefinger into his mouth. He was clean except for the powdery dust on his feet, and he smelled of baby shampoo. Somebody must have bathed and dressed him not too long ago.

DanDan briefly held the piece of pipe out for me to see.

'What you got there?' I asked. He snatched it back, then bent over and ran it through the sand in the driveway.

'Big truck!' he said, and made roaring noises.

'Where's Tunes?' I asked again.

'Brrrarrrrrum, brarrrarrrum,' said DanDan.

I straightened in time to see Tunes amble around the corner of the house in her cutoff blue jeans and a T-shirt, DanDan's little cousin Kali balanced on her hip.

'Buck Smith, what're you doing here? Jep comes home and finds you, you'll be sorry you came.' She laughed. Something in the way I stood there tongue-tied made her stop. 'What's the matter with you?'

I was still having a hard time getting my mouth going. I ran up to her and took Kali from her. Kali's plump little arms went around my neck. She smelled of milk and baby powder.

'You best get yourself going,' I said. 'Sheriff's found your gun. He's looking for you to take you in. Kneebone told him he hadn't seen you since last night. He's with Sheriff. Reckon Sheriff didn't want him to come warning you. He just left our house a few minutes ago, I think he was going to look around the farm before coming here. I came the back way, but he could be here any second. I'll stay here with the babies. Go!'

Tunes hesitated just a second. Her eyes narrowed.

'Mazie'll be back shortly,' she said. 'She's buying groceries. There's stuff boiling on the stove.' Tunes' arms rose at her sides, just as they'd done before she jumped out of the skiff the day we'd found Jorge.

'I'll get it,' I said. 'Take my bike.'

But she was gone, headed through the woods, down toward the north side of the neck, the opposite direction from where our farm was. I still remember seeing the pale bottoms of her bare feet as she disappeared at a dead run into the woods, and I wondered with a sick heart what her gun was doing out where Sheriff could find it and when I'd see her again.

Mazie came back from the grocery store a few minutes later in Jep's old pickup, which rattled down the track before coughing to a stop. I told Mazie what I knew in a distracted way, because I wanted to get away before Sheriff caught me there. I took the plastic grocery sack out of Mazie's one hand and held Kali out to her. Kali's little hands opened and closed with excitement when she saw her grandmama.

'Dear Lord,' Mazie said, shaking her head.

'Tunes'll be okay,' I said. 'I got to go before Sheriff gets here.'

Mazie took the grocery sack back and flicked her wrist at me, shooing me away, then scurried for the house, her head ducked as if it'd started to rain.

I was halfway out Mazie's driveway when I heard Sheriff's wagon turn in. I pulled the bicycle off the dirt track and threw myself down beside it in the tall grass. A stiff breeze ruffled through where I'd walked, fluffing up the weeds and erasing the marks I'd left almost instantly. When Sheriff'd passed round another bend and out of sight, I pushed the bike back on to the track and pedalled for all I was worth.

But I wasn't halfway home on the back road when Dad came flying along in the truck. He stopped so fast when he saw me the truck lurched. He got out, his face set in a dark frown. He picked up my bicycle in one hand and flung it into the back of the truck.

'Get in,' was all he said. We drove back along the way I'd come, back to Mazie's where Sheriff's white wagon sat, one wheel in Mazie's flower bed near the front door. The lights still flashed blue and red, and both doors on the driver's side stood open.

Mazie was just as I'd left her, Kali on one hip, holding the bag of groceries. DanDan stood against her leg, his hand grasping a fold in the skirt of her housedress. Kneebone stood beside Mazie, and Sheriff looked madder'n a hissy goose.

'Buck warned her,' Dad said. He pushed me forward roughly, like I was a prisoner.

Sheriff's eyes narrowed and he hooked his thumbs in his belt loops.

'Why'd you do that?' he asked, his voice dangerously quiet. 'You know I could arrest you for being an accessory after the fact.'

'She didn't do it, Sheriff,' I said, my voice calm.

'That's not for you to say,' Sheriff said, his lower jaw working on a blade of grass. 'You best take him home and not let him out of your sight, Senior,' Sheriff said to Dad.

That morning Dad was as upset as I'd ever seen him. He took me down to the barn, which was idle during the planting season, when all the action began to focus on the packing shed.

It started to rain, gently at first, as Dad paced in front of the stall in the barn's dim light. The rain fell harder until a few moments later it beat like fury and the sound on the tin roof was sharp as thunder.

I expected a good tanning, but Dad paced and paced, muttering to himself. He kept starting out with what I knew would be a lecture. But he couldn't seem to find the words to go on. I could barely hear his muttering through the hammer of the rain.

'Why'd you do it, son?' he began several times.

At first I just couldn't answer him. The enormity of what I'd just done was beginning to sink in, and I was scared – scared I'd end up doing Tunes more harm than good, scared I'd be arrested, too. My throat began to ache, and I was no longer able to keep the tears back.

'I was afraid Tunes'd go to jail. I know she didn't do it, Dad! And I was afraid Jumbo'd get her,' I said finally, trying to calm my breathing so I could talk.

'Son, this isn't something for you to deal with. You'd better leave proving or disproving who did what to Sheriff.' He walked in circles, his hands jammed in the back pockets of his jeans. He made no move to comfort me, though I was crying like a baby, tears dripping off my nose and chin.

'Buck, you got to let go of Tunes,' he said finally, getting to what he really had on his mind.

'Dad, she's most likely in real danger!' I swiped the back of my hand across my face. 'You'd never abandon a friend in trouble. Why are you taking Mr Rawlin's word over Tunes'?' I wiped my nose on the bottom of my T-shirt.

It was dark outside, with the storm gathering itself up for another strike, and I felt like there was a darkness inside me, too. My father, who'd taught me right from wrong since I was a baby, was telling me something I knew wasn't right. I just couldn't accept that, and I intended to keep arguing the point, way past knowing it was fruitless.

'We're not talking about Tunes, son,' he said. 'We're talking about you and your safety. Tunes's done wrong, Buck. She's in a right smart load of trouble, and there's nothing you can do to help her out of it. She's broken the law, and –'

'No she hasn't!' I shouted.

'Jumbo told Sheriff he saw Jorge and Tunes together Friday night,' Dad said, holding his hand up for me to be quiet. In the grey flat light he looked old and tired, his hair grey, skin colourless. 'Jumbo and Menendez saw her down by the labour camp, the same time you said she was out netting bait with you. And now finding her gun in Little Creek . . . It looks real bad, Buck.'

'I'm sure there's some explanation about her gun, Dad. That's what you said when I told you about Mr Rawlin out lookin' for the body . . .'

'Lord knows,' Dad said, looking close to despair, 'after your fiddling with the truth, Sheriff was going to take Jumbo's word over yours.'

I didn't say anything. I realized he was right. It would've been better if I'd just stuck with the truth. I sank to a new depth of misery.

'She and Jorge had some kind of spat,' Dad went on. 'Jorge smacked her, and then he put his arms around her. Menendez saw the whole thing, too. After that they went off together.' Menendez helped Jorge maintain the labour camps, but I knew he was jealous of Jorge. And I'd've bet Menendez would say anything Jumbo told him to say.

'It's a lie!' I shouted through my tears and above the roar of the rain on the roof, the thunder rolling above that.

'Don't you talk about lying!' Dad said. He was madder'n I ever saw him. 'You've been telling nothing but lies!'

'But it's not true there was any romance between Tunes and Jorge! I'd swear my life on it, Dad.'

'Menendez and Mr Rawlin said Tunes and Jorge had been seeing each other since January. They said everybody knew about it, Buck.'

'I don't believe it!' I said. 'First, how could somebody Tunes' size hit a person hard enough to break his head?

And second, Jorge wouldn't . . . He loved Tunes and me like we were his own kids.'

'Buck, I know it's hard for you to think Jorge did anything wrong. He was good to you. But that kind of thing can make a man do strange things – things that are otherwise out of character. Sheriff thinks maybe Jorge was jealous and Tunes might have killed him by accident, in self-defence. Sheriff says if Tunes hit Jorge the right way with something heavy enough she could've done him that kind of injury.'

'Mr Rawlin's trying to make it appear Tunes killed Jorge,' I said. 'Can't you see that? He's smart, Dad. Why can't you see?'

'Son, it doesn't look good for Tunes. Sheriff believes Jumbo. I hate to say it, but everything Jumbo's said so far makes sense. It would take a powerful lot to explain it all away, let along charge Jumbo and make it stand up in a court of law.'

'And what about Tunes? She's a good person. You've known Tunes since she was born. Why do you believe Mr Rawlin instead of her? He's not a good person. Are you scared of him just like everybody else?'

'It's not easy to know right from wrong, son,' he said. I began to protest, but he held up his hand.

'Let me finish. It's not a matter of taking sides,' he said. He sounded weary. I didn't wonder, the way he kept on with an argument he knew was full of holes. He'd stopped pacing, and looked at me level, like I was an adult.

'I want you to put a right smart lot of distance between you and Tunes.'

'She's my best friend and she's in trouble.'

'Son, the trouble is the main reason, but it isn't the only thing. Even if Tunes gets clear of this, she's reaching an age where she's interested in things other than fishing and hunting and sitting out on the creeks with you.

Sometimes it takes boys longer than girls to mature, but –'

'Dad, that won't matter between Tunes 'n' me. We already talked about it.'

He was quiet for a bit. I thought for a few minutes maybe he understood after all, and I wondered whether I dared hope . . .

'You should have other friends, Buck, boys and girls. When you start to be interested in girls, I hope it'll be girls you have more in common with –'

'There's nobody in the world I have more in common with than Tunes!' I said. 'And we're not talking about me and "girls". We're talking about Tunes.'

'I just don't want to see you hurt,' he said. He looked miserable, like he wasn't sure he wanted to be saying what he'd just said. It sounded like something Mama might've put him up to.

I was filled with puzzlement. I'd expected a good hiding at least for lying and helping Tunes get away. But what ate at me was that suddenly Dad didn't even seem to care about Tunes. And then without warning another wave of grief for Jorge washed over me. Jorge would never have a say about the charge that he'd been messing with Tunes – or about anything else – ever again.

Since I'd caused some of Tunes' difficulties by lying, I felt desperately responsible for proving she hadn't killed Jorge, and helping to find whoever did. I knew I'd need help, most likely from an adult, someone who knew about the law. I was incredulous that help wouldn't be coming from Dad. And angry, suddenly very angry. And then it came to me.

'Judge!' I shouted. 'He'll help us. Judge cares about her and he cares about me. He was Jorge's friend!'

'Buck,' Dad said slowly, 'Jorge was my friend, too. But we have to leave finding who killed him up to Sheriff.' He looked troubled, and I was glad. I'd meant to hurt him.

'And you know as well as I do Judge has dropped his sails,' Dad said. That made me even angrier. Judge'd had another of his spells about a week before. He'd got lost again, this time overnight, and his wife and son wouldn't let him take the boat out any more. Said he'd lost his faculties.

'Judge's not near as addled as folks make him out to be,' I said hotly. 'If you won't help Tunes and me, we have to find somebody who will . . .'

'I don't want to hear another word about Tunes,' Dad said. 'You're not to leave the farm until some of this is cleared up. I don't want you to go anywhere – by land or water – until I say you can.'

Then he stopped talking, although I didn't think we'd finished. There was a lot to what he said I didn't understand and didn't think he really meant. He was being so unjust. It wasn't a bit like him.

'Why, Dad? Why? Answer me!'

But he turned his back and headed his big old work boots toward the house. If he'd given up on me, I surely had given up on him. I was all in a turmoil. I kicked a corner of the horse stall, and a right smart pain shot up my shin.

Chapter 10

Mama and Dad kept a close watch over me. They made sure I was so busy I couldn't leave the house except for school. I felt like a prisoner, up to my elbows in soapsuds after every meal and keeping company with Mama and Gran while they cleaned and worked in the garden.

They all seemed to enjoy it, though I couldn't think why. I was completely preoccupied with visions of Tunes huddled wet and shivering somewhere on one of the creeks.

In school I became a loner like Tunes'd been. I had no heart for hoops and talk with Dewey Morgan or anybody else for that matter. I refused to let anyone gossip about Tunes in my range of hearing. After a while they left me alone. I just put in my time and came home every day.

The weather stayed coolish and grey and inhospitable. The water and land looked alike, both flat and dull, and the sky above pressed down heavy like the plate of an iron until it seemed nothing could move. And I felt the weight of being caught between.

Obie hung out on the doorstep, waiting for someone to take him down to the water, or down the lane, or anywhere. Every once in a while he'd get tired of waiting around and he'd head down toward the dock. He'd return a few minutes later dripping wet. He'd lie down on the step again and wait some more.

Mama and Gran were doing their spring house-cleaning. Mama had me take the mattresses off the beds on Saturday and vacuum the box springs and frames.

For some reason, the combination of cleaning and grey weather put Mama in a good frame of mind, and she chirped happily away all day, talking about the charity ball coming up and what various ladies were contributing in the way of flowers. I sneezed and my eyes smarted with all the dust, but she paid me no mind.

I began to grow impatient and restless, and took to pacing when I wasn't working, until Gran couldn't stand it.

'Land sakes alive,' she said one afternoon. 'You'd think you were afflicted with a passel of fleas. Here, help peel these potatoes, settle yourself down.'

Mama had her bridge club over for lunch and an afternoon of cards. We had the day off from school for teachers' meetings. I wanted to avoid Mama's friends and stay outside, so I gave Obie a bath. The fleas had become near-epidemic, and Obie'd been scratching a right lot. For a dog who loved water he sure hated a bath. He stood quivering, his head down like he was sick. Soon as I finished he took off at a dead run, straight down to the water, where he rolled in a mess of dead fish until he smelled awful enough to be to his own liking again.

I took my fishing rod down and cast off the dock for about a half hour but didn't catch anything. I was starving. Finally there was nothing left for me to do but go to the kitchen and get a peanut butter sandwich. I slipped in the back door and tiptoed around without being found out.

The ladies talked and laughed loudly in the garden room just beside the kitchen.

'The only thing I can think to do is ask her to wear a uniform,' somebody, it sounded like Mrs Dixon, said. 'But you can't get them to wear uniforms these days. Lorena used to wear that nice grey one with the starched white collar and apron. Now she wears whatever she pleases.'

'It's the attitude I don't like,' Mama's friend Mrs Thales said. 'Last week Cherelle came to work wearing a T-shirt that had "It's a Black Thing" written on the front. Now, what's that supposed to mean.'

Listening to them go on about the folks who worked in their houses made my blood boil. I took my sandwich and a glass of milk out to the garden.

I sat on the old wrought-iron garden bench that looked out over the roses and down to the creek beyond. I felt so alone. I missed Tunes, and Mama and Dad might just as well have been on a trip somewheres. They didn't talk to me about anything. They just talked around things, and I found myself doing the same thing.

'You're having a rough time of it, aren't you, boy?' It was Gran, in her rubber gardening clogs and her blue coverall, with her straw hat, a clutch of violets pinned to the band. She was wheeling a barrowload to the mulch pile. I nodded. She set down her load and sat beside me.

'Your daddy's being awfully tough on you,' she said.

'It's not that, Gran,' I said. We looked out at a heron flying past, large, awkward, and ancient-looking, like a prehistoric thing moving in slow motion. 'I was wrong. I lied. But they're acting contrary to everything they ever taught me. Dad turning his back on Tunes, Mama being all sweet and friendly with Jumbo Rawlin. I don't understand!'

'Buck, honey,' Gran said, turning toward me. I looked into her sharp blue eyes. 'In your long life you'll see a lot of hypocrisy and people being wrong about things. Now, your daddy's no hypocrite. But it's awful hard to see your own mama and daddy being wrong about something important.'

'They've known Tunes all her life. It's almost like they were turning their backs on me!'

She held up her hand. It was calloused and crusted with garden dirt, like a man's.

'They're human, child,' she said. 'You've got to forgive them. You've got to learn that people make mistakes and think wrong even with the best of intentions. You've got to learn not to let it break your heart.'

'But you're not . . .'

'I'm old and wise all right,' Gran said with a twinkle. She patted my arm. 'I also don't have a lot of influence around here.' She looked out over the creek, and she seemed tired. I wondered whether she'd had words with Mama and Dad about the business with Tunes.

'Come on,' she said. 'I'll fix you some real food to eat.'

That cheered me some, because I knew she meant ham biscuits, and there wasn't a thing I liked better in the world.

Through the hopelessness and pain, a plan began to take shape in my mind, without my even knowing I was thinking on it. It was a kind of realization at first, then it grew into a wild hope that seemed unlikely, and then when I got down to it, likely as all get-out.

The realization was I had two options: I could think the worst, let things take the course Jumbo'd planned, and act as helpless as I felt to prove Tunes was innocent.

Or I could be more optimistic and do something.

After that became clear, I was able to concentrate on how to get away and find Tunes and straighten out this terrible, awful mess.

I needed to get to Judge, I thought. That was my best hope. While it was true Judge had his 'spells', they didn't last very long, and afterward he didn't seem to remember he'd done or said something that didn't make sense. And I was convinced folks made more of it than they should have.

One thing about the Eastern Shore, so isolated and remote, everybody knew everybody else. And that was a fish that swam both ways. When Judge went missing, half the county turned out to look for him. On the other hand, everybody clucked their tongues now, sayin' poor Judge, once a wise man, lost his wits. He was old – what'd folks expect?

But fact was Judge knew about the law, and I believed he was more capable than folks gave him credit for. Once I found Tunes, Judge would help us work out how to prove it was Jumbo killed Jorge. If it turned out he couldn't help, I told myself I'd deal with that later.

I worked like a demon that weekend, banging dust out of cushions, taking down drapes, airing them, hanging them up again. My mind hardly knew what my body was doing, I was so consumed with plotting details.

The weather cleared, and Mama and Gran and I moved on out to the garden. We loosened the soil around the roses, turning the warm earth with our bare hands. We worked in manure, sprayed the rose bushes, and mulched them with shatters that fell from the tall old pines down by the water.

All the while I was building a stash in the barn to take to Tunes once I'd found her. Every day after school I went into the pantry and took a can of vegetables or a can of fruit or some ham, and hid it away until I had a chance to take it down to the barn. I found an old blanket with an elk's head design in its centre in Gran's linen closet. I felt like a squirrel, but nothing could divert me from planning my first trip out to look for Tunes and deliver her supplies.

I didn't complain about the hard work. Every once in a while I'd think of Jumbo catching up with Tunes and I'd have to put the wheelbarrow down right where I stood and say a little prayer for her, that she'd be safe wherever she was, and that I'd be able to find her.

Mama and Gran and Dad carried on as if everything was normal, listening to public radio around the kitchen table at suppertime, discussing a book or politics while we ate. Now it was daylight savings time Dad went back out to the fields while I helped Mama and Gran wash up.

It gave me time to think. Sometimes Mama or Dad would look at me and ask why I was so quiet. They'd always encouraged me to have opinions, and I'd always been happy to offer them. But those days I'd just shrug, and there'd be an uncomfortable silence for a while, until Gran changed the subject and asked Dad about something, like the new irrigation system he was installing in the north field.

I didn't see much of Kneebone. He and Dad were getting the packing shed ready for an early harvest of cucumbers. He walked around as usual, not saying much. He used to drop in every morning for a cup of coffee with Dad to talk about what they were going to do that day. But after Tunes disappeared he stopped doing that.

By the next weekend I began to lose heart. They hadn't presented me with one opportunity to get away. I felt I'd been wasting my time. No way was Dad going to let me out of his sight long enough to go hunting for Tunes. I felt defeated.

Just as I was thinking that, I looked up to see the bald eagle rise from the edge of the creek with a big eel curled and writhing darkly around his yellow feet. That eel was so heavy the eagle had to make an exaggerated effort, heaving his wings for all he was worth to lift off. Once up, he soared flat and easy against the sky, like there was no extra weight at all. How I envied him, saying to all the world: Nobody has anything on me. I can do as I wish.

Then a flock of crows spotted the eagle and hovered flapping above him in a clump. As if at a signal, one tucked in his wings and dived at the eagle, followed by a second crow; then one by one they dive-bombed him, as if they'd agreed beforehand on an elaborate strategy. The eagle heaved his mighty wings once more to halt his loss of altitude, but with the eel he couldn't get up and away. The wind carried the crows' gleeful cackles to me, and they began to dive faster, taking turns until the eagle flinched and feinted to one side.

When it became evident that there was no getting away from the crows, the eagle dropped the eel, which fell almost at my feet. Within a second the crows were upon it, their voices turning to querulous croaks and screeches that mounted until the eel was in enough pieces for each crow to fly away with a chunk. The eagle was nowhere to be seen.

Isn't that something, I thought to myself. Even the freest of the free can't do exactly as he pleases.

Chapter 11

All along I'd been thinking it was only a matter of time before Dad would praise me for my good behaviour and tell me I could go down to Bartons' or over to see Kneebone or just get out on the dock to fish for a while.

He had to know the heat was getting to me. It raised itself up from the earth in shimmery waves and prickled at my skin like drying salt water. He knew me well enough to imagine I wanted to go for a swim, to kick back and float among the sea meadows. I'd done that every day of my life that the temperature rose above eighty degrees.

I'd been doing my best to act like a boy who'd learned his lesson well. Why wouldn't he let up on me?

I didn't need much time. I had a strong hunch where Tunes was hiding out. We had a secret place we hadn't been to since the fall before, when we'd had the run-in with Jumbo out on Little Creek. About two summers earlier, Tunes and I had been out in one of the creek's tiny harbours when we saw a family of otters playing around under the duck blind that stood abandoned up in the farthest reach of the inlet.

We got to hiding out in the blind, trying to entice those slick little animals with a bucket of croakers. We stretched our arms out, holding the fish through the hole in the floor. At first the otters dived for the bottom the second they saw us. But there's nothing curiouser than an otter, and it wasn't long before they stood up and cocked their heads, fixing us with their bright black eyes, their noses twitching every which way. Soon after, they'd take the fish right from our hands, and once they even let us sit in the water next to them while they played.

The mouth of the inlet was hidden by overhanging branches and the water was shoal up there, so nobody ever came along. It was our favourite hidey-hole that summer and the next. Until the incident with Jumbo, that is, and then we were afraid to go back.

The duck blind was only ten minutes away from where the skiff was padlocked down behind the barn. My plan was to take the hacksaw from Dad's shop to cut through the chain and relock it with one of the other padlocks Dad kept in the shop. That way he wouldn't know I'd taken the skiff out.

But Dad walked around with his jaw set like a boulder and his shoulders hunched, and never gave me a chance to get away. He or Mama came to the soybean field every morning to drop me off for school. Said it was so I wouldn't be lonely waiting for the bus myself. But I knew it was to be sure I got on every day.

Mama relaxed a little after school let out for the summer. But they didn't show any sign of relenting, making sure that I had chores around the farm that would keep me busy every minute.

The only reason I could think Dad would be so vigilant was that he was afraid for me. It was the only thing that made sense. The fact that he wouldn't help Kneebone look for Tunes – even when he thought she might have done something terrible wrong – was not like him at all.

That Saturday my chance came. It was steamy, and I'd dug in the rose garden until I was blinded by sweat, widening the bed outside the dining room so Mama could add some new varieties. Kneebone showed up, his shirt stuck to his back. He'd walked over to our place, which was unusual for him.

'Where's your truck, Kneebone?' Dad asked. Dad was dressed in his new work clothes, which meant he was fixing to go somewheres.

'Mired over on the far side of 'rigation pond, sir,' Kneebone said. 'Need the tractor to pull me out.'

'I was just on my way over across the Bay to get some spare parts for that new irrigation system,' Dad said.

He looked at me and frowned, like he was deciding whether to trust me. 'Buck can come over on the tractor and pull you out.' Then he turned to me.

'Buck, I want you back here soon's Kneebone's truck is out. I'll be back in about two hours. Understand?' I nodded, but I knew there was no way he could get across the Bay, do his errand, and get back home in less than three hours. Then Dad looked up at Kneebone. 'Keep him out of trouble, Kneebone. He's not to leave the farm.'

'Yessir,' said Kneebone. 'Yessir.'

It wasn't exactly the chance I'd been waiting for because Mama and Gran would expect me to be back as soon as I'd hauled Kneebone's truck out. But at least it was a chance to get out from under Dad's stern watch for a time and to talk to Kneebone. Anything was welcome after being shut up with my family.

Kneebone and I walked together toward the barn without talking. I was dying to ask if he'd heard from Tunes. I knew well and good he and Jep had been out looking for her. I would have heard if they'd found her, I felt sure. But I was so sick with worry I wanted to learn something – anything! Knowing Kneebone, I felt the most productive thing I could do was wait for him to speak.

Once we'd rounded the garden shed and were on the weedy path to the barn and out of Dad's sight, Kneebone put his hand on my shoulder and left it there as we walked. Obie trotted along behind us.

Finally I could wait no longer.

'Kneebone,' I said, my voice coming out all breathless, like I was winded. 'You got to tell me. Have you heard anything from her? Found any trace of her?'

Kneebone didn't answer, and my patience gave out completely.

'You got to tell me, Kneebone. I been near to crazy with worry! Every second, sleeping and waking, all I can think of is Tunes.'

Still he didn't speak, just walked along worrying a piece of grass in the side of his mouth, his knobbly hand still on my shoulder as we passed the low wooden beehives beyond the barn, down toward the rough-board shed where the tractor was.

As we passed the bees I remembered to snatch the red baseball cap off my head and hide it under my T-shirt. Last summer Tunes had more than thirty stings because she wore red shorts one day as we ran past the hives on our way to see if the blue heron fledglings were still in the rookery at the edge of the creek.

Then Dad's truck shot by on the oystershell road the other side of the field, sending up pale grey showers of dust. A few minutes later I heard another car, and looked up to see Mama and Gran, all gussed up for a fancy lunch, riding in Mama's old silver sedan. I remembered it was some special garden club day, and hope sprang into my heart for the first time in weeks as I realized this might be my chance after all.

'I know your daddy's been keeping a keen eye on you,' Kneebone said finally. 'You been havin' no chance to look out for Tunes. Me and Jep go out every morning, soon's sun's up. We haven't seen a tick off 'a her.'

I'd thought about telling Kneebone to look in the duck blind. But I knew full well that if Tunes'd wanted him to find her, she would've arranged for him to stumble on her those mornings he was out. So I took my turn keeping quiet.

I wanted to tell Kneebone I was angry and confused and disgusted with Dad for not going with him to find her. I thought he must feel worse about it than I did. Kneebone'd been loyal to our family like his father had been to my grandfather, and more generations on both sides before that. And he treated me like a son. If I was lost and in trouble, first one out to find me would be Kneebone.

Suddenly I recognized that the hot-all-over, tongue-tied feeling I had was nothing but shame. I was right ashamed that my father hadn't honoured Kneebone's loyalty, and there wasn't a thing I could do about it without dishonouring Dad.

I'd learned a lot from Kneebone and his silences over the years. When there wasn't anything you could say, it was best not to say anything at all. But I was trembly as a new fawn and near to tears as we started up the tractor and turned out into the field.

Kneebone stood on the back of the tractor, letting me drive toward the newly ploughed field that lay between us and the irrigation pond, its rows so straight and narrow you could see clear down them, a quarter mile.

By the time we were out of the trees a swarm of gulls had gathered behind us, waiting for the tractor to plough up more worms and crickets to dive for. Obie busied himself by running at the gulls full tilt, scaring them up in a cloud only to settle farther on just behind the tractor, where he'd turn and run at them again. The gull game was one of his favourites, and he could play it all day.

'Reverend King Saloman Jones is getting together a group of churchmen to go out after Tunes,' Kneebone said, leaning over my shoulder and shouting so I could hear him above the tractor's engine. The gulls swooped low over our heads, as if to menace us into digging up something for them to eat. I heard an edge of something

I couldn't identify in Kneebone's voice, and I turned to look at him.

What Kneebone said next'd like to take the wind out of my sails.

'I know you got a mind to go out looking for her yourself, Buck,' he said. 'Don't do it. I don't want you to.'

I'd been just about to shift gears, and my foot slipped off the clutch as I whirled round to face him. The tractor jerked to a standstill, and Kneebone lurched sideways. The gulls swooped even lower. Kneebone looked out across the field. 'It'd just make trouble for us and for you and your daddy. Reverend King Saloman Jones said they'd stop lookin' if any white folks got involved. So please. Don't come lookin'.'

That just about did it. Something powerful strange was going on here. First Dad saying he wanted me and Tunes to stay apart before she'd even had her say, and now Kneebone.

'You know I'm ten times more likely to find her than the Reverend King Saloman Jones,' I said, still incredulous. 'Did Dad ask you to talk to me?'

He stood for a long ten seconds, balanced behind me on the tractor, looking out across the field.

'No, Buck, he didn't. But if he told you to stay away, it was good advice.'

'Kneebone,' I said, all mixed up with anger and helplessness, 'what's got into you and Dad? Both of you taught me and Tunes about doing the right thing, being loyal and truthful. Why're you changing now Tunes is in trouble?'

'Folks just reach a place where they got to do what's best for their own, Buck,' Kneebone said, his voice weary. 'Your daddy wants to do best by you, and I want to do best by Tunes.'

I stared at him for a few moments.

'Well, I always thought I was your own!' I said, my voice rising. 'If that's how you feel, haul out your own damn truck!' I jumped down from the tractor. I hit the ground at a tear and ran across the furrows, leaving Kneebone standing there with the tractor stalled and his mouth open, and Obie panting to catch up.

I ran all the way back to the driveway, my feet flying over the furrows, each footstep skidding in the soft ploughed earth, all the way to the barn. Obie ran on ahead, and I wondered as he ducked in through the barnyard how he knew where I was headed. I ran to the back, where Dad's shop was, and without a thought went straight to where the hacksaw hung on a nail. In the pile of cables and chains and screws in the shop bench drawer lay the assortment of padlocks he kept on hand, each with its own key.

In the old tack room, dusty and cobwebby from the years since we'd had horses, I gathered up the bag of food, some T-shirts and shorts from the vast collection in my dresser drawer, the blanket, an old denim jacket and some other supplies, and ran with my arms loaded and the hacksaw clutched in my fist through the barn toward the south door.

Just inside the big sliding door on the southern wall of the barn, hanging on a hook, was Gran's old gardening hat, pale yellow straw with a sagging wide brim and the violets, now wilted and grey. Beneath it on the same hook hung her faded blue gardening coverall, which she tied over her dress when she worked outside. I hesitated just a second before snatching them both up and stuffing them into the provision bags. If anybody saw the skiff out on the creek, I could put on Gran's things and they would think it was my dear old grandmother, who often lit out to see her old friend Mrs Mabrey over across the creek.

I fairly skidded down the path to the back side of the neck, Obie hot on my heels. The skiff stood in the little cove off the inlet, just where I'd padlocked it on Dad's orders, water nudging friendly and soft at its stern. The heavy chain lay glinting, half draped in the water.

Obie leapt into the bow and sat grinning broadly. I knew he couldn't figure out why we'd been away from the water so long.

I checked the gas tank. Half-full. I applied the hacksaw to the chain and put the cut links into my pocket with the padlock. In no time I was poling the skiff out toward the creek. Before leaving the lee of the bank, I threw the old lock and cut chain links into the deeper water, pulled on Gran's coverall, and tied the wide faded blue ribbon of her hat under my chin.

I was so keyed up I felt I could hardly keep myself inside my skin. Doing something was a thousand times better than doing nothing, and I got a right smart lot of satisfaction out of being there with the sun on my back and the breeze skinning over my face.

Once out on the creek, I hauled on the starter rope, and the engine sang to life. I opened the throttle full and kept it there. About halfway down the creek, Doke's wife, Dora, came aputtering along in Doke's old skiff and set my heart to hammering. Sure's spring she'd want to sit and jaw with Gran, so I raised my hand and waved a bit regretfully, as if I was sorry I didn't have time to chat, and tilted my head to keep my face shaded by the brim. Dora waved enthusiastically and went on past.

I fairly held my breath the rest of the way until I turned the skiff from the creek and into the Bay, then down into Little Creek to Jumbo's inlet with Obie leaning into the turns. There I cut the engine dead. My heart was still thumping wildly against my ribs, for it was no secret I was disallowed out on the water, and nobody would have hesitated to tell Dad if they saw me.

Carefully and deliberately I hugged the shade of the far shore of the inlet and poled up to just behind the duck blind. I pulled the skiff under it, and Tunes poked her head down through the hole in the floor.

'Sure am glad I wasn't waitin' on you to eat,' said Tunes. Obie's tail whacked the floorboards of the skiff with joy. Tunes pulled her head back through, and Obie levitated clear off his haunches and leapt through the duck blind floor. I poked my head through, knocking Gran's hat askew. Obie set on Tunes' face and neck with his big pink tongue.

I dangled there, Gran's hat held to the side of my head by the ribbon caught over my ears, my legs still hanging over the skiff, before I could get myself up through the hole. I didn't even have the sense to feel foolish, I was so close to bursting with happiness.

Chapter 12

When Tunes saw me she let out a hoot I was afraid they'd hear clear down to Eastville. She grabbed ahold of her stomach and fell over on her side and gave way to laughing so hard I thought sure she'd be sick.

'Why didn't you let somebody find you before now?' I asked, a little put out, now I knew she was safe after being so afraid for her. I hauled my legs up after me, sat on the edge of the hole, and disentangled myself from the hat and its ribbons.

'Why'd you wait so long to come lookin'?' she asked, her eyes snapping for an instant before she collapsed again, helpless with laughter. I looked around a bit to give her a chance to get over her foolishness.

The blind was right homey, with a clutch of purple pickerelweed in a tin can on a little stand under the window, and beside the bouquet her slingshot. Tunes had propped up a shutter on one side just a bit to let in some air and light. From outside it looked shut up tighter than a tick, with reeds growing up all around it.

She must have sneaked back home to fetch some things, like her slingshot, while Kneebone was away. Her old worn athletic shoes sat on the floor under the closed-up opposite window, which faced onto the side of the inlet behind Jumbo's property. I'd'a wagered she hadn't had them on since she fetched them. Her toes and the sides of her feet were cracked, like they'd had hard use, and streaked with bay muck.

Kneebone's camp stove and a bottle of alcohol fuel with a rag stuffed in as a stopper stood under the window alongside her shoes.

I couldn't think what more to say, so I hugged Tunes' neck, and she hugged mine back. When she let go, she snuffled once, then snatched away the bags of provisions I'd hauled up behind me so I wouldn't see her eyes were damp. By then I was grinning at her like a dozen fools.

All the while Obie was dancing and hopping from front legs to back, trying to lick every available inch of both of us. His teeth clacked together like a doddering old man's. His throat emitted happy whines, and his tongue was like a wringing-wet washcloth.

'What you been eating all this time?' I asked. The place was clean and neat as Kneebone's house. It almost felt like it should have the same blue-and-white checkered curtains at the windows.

Tunes hunted greedily through the bags I'd brought. Suddenly I felt hungry as a bear, too, and we dug out a package of lemon cream waffle biscuits to share.

'Oh, I been slingshootin' rabbits and fishin',' Tunes said, her mouth full of lemon cream. 'Caught more fish than I could eat.'

'How'd you catch 'em?' I asked. She cut her eyes sideways at me, as if trying to decide whether to let me in on a secret.

'You sneak up real slow and quiet on a fishy-looking place in shoal water, lay your hand way down amongst the weeds, and wait for a lunker to swim near you. Let him drift right into the cup of your hand, then wiggle your fingers real slow and gentle until they're just barely touching his belly. He'll stay still and you can catch him with your bare hands.'

'Where'd you learn that?'

'My granddaddy,' she said, looking right smug. 'And there's lots of wild asparagus and fennel and berries along the banks. I been eating just fine!'

'Sheriff been out here looking for you?' I asked then.

'Police boats've been up and down this creek every day and most nights, playing their searchlights all up and down the banks,' she said. 'Only come here the back of this neck once, and then they got hung up on a shoal a coupla hundred feet down. They didn't come up far enough to even see the duck blind.'

Obie's head was in Tunes' lap. He was near as much her dog as mine, for the time we'd spent together ever since he was a pup. She stroked his soft ears and down his nose. He licked at her hand every time it passed in the vicinity of his tongue, and made soft whiny noises. His tail kept up a steady thump as we talked.

I told Tunes all the things I hadn't had time to tell her the day I came to Mazie's to warn her Sheriff was coming for her. I rushed on, talking faster'n my tongue could go, telling her what-all had happened since she'd disappeared that day, which seemed ages ago, although it'd only been a couple of weeks.

Only time she reacted was when I said how worried Kneebone'd been and how the Reverend King Saloman Jones had mounted a search party. Then she thumped her knee and hooted again.

'Kneebone sure must be worried to let that old Reverend Toad come looking!' she shouted, and I tried to shush her. 'They-all sure never will find me, cuz I can hear that man slappin' his lips together two creeks away!'

I laughed with her for a minute. It felt good, like when you've been underwater almost too long, then come up for a breath of air. We both quieted down after a bit and sat for a moment, each with our own thoughts.

I told her then how her daddy and mine had been acting so strange, like they wanted us to give up on each other. The shame I'd felt talking with Kneebone came over me again, burning the back of my neck and the rims of my ears until they were right painful.

'Dad said once Sheriff had your gun the evidence fell into place,' I said. 'How'd your gun get in Little Creek, anyway, Tunes?'

She shrugged her shoulders, but she seemed to be concentrating hard on pulling a tick from under Obie's chin. He rolled over and let her pick at him.

'I told Dad there was an explanation,' I said. I hoped she'd offer it up, but still she said nothing.

So I told her what Jumbo and Menendez had told Sheriff about seeing her with Jorge over by the labour camp.

'All those Mexican workers are terrified of Jumbo,' I said. 'Menendez would say anything Jumbo told him to say.' Tunes sat still as a pool of deep water.

'I need to get away, Buck,' she said after a bit.

'You're safe here for now,' I said, knowing I was right. 'Besides, if you left the Shore and Sheriff caught up with you, he'd think you did it for sure. That would be crazy – '

'Don't you say crazy, Buck! I been sitting here waiting for you these last weeks, not knowing what-all was happening. I been thinking long and hard about what I need to do. I need to get off the Shore. And there's not an ounce of crazy to it!' Her eyes glinted yellow and fierce. 'Just what d'you think I can accomplish sitting here waiting some more . . . waiting for what?'

'Well, I'm thinking if we had some help, maybe we could prove it was Jumbo killed Jorge. Then Sheriff'd have to let you go, and things could be like they were before.'

'Hmph!' she said, hunching up her shoulders as if she felt all alone in the world except for one Buck Smith, who'd never been anything save too naïve to understand

115

the gravity of her problems. And that put my back up, because I *did* understand. Or at least I was pretty sure I did.

'There's one person can help,' I said. She glared, waiting. 'Judge. Everybody thinks Judge Wickham's gone soft between the ears. Nobody'd suspect he'd be able to help us – or even that we'd ask him!'

Tunes sat still for a moment. Her eyes looked kind of wild, like she'd reverted to relyin' on her animal instincts.

'You know nobody believes Judge any more,' she said. 'How's he going to help?'

'Advice, to begin with,' I said. 'Give me one day. Let me talk to him, see what he has to say. I'll come back tonight. I swear.'

'Don't you tell him where I am!'

'But we can trust Judge!' I said.

'There's nobody I trust,' she said, and folded her arms across her chest. 'Come back tonight. And you can't say where I am.'

'Okay,' I said. 'But you got to trust me, Tunes. What if I can't come until tomorrow?'

She shook her head, and I knew she'd be gone if I didn't come that night.

'Okay,' I said. 'I'll be back.' She held one hand up and I slapped her palm. But it was without much enthusiasm that she did it.

'Well,' I said, reluctant to leave, 'I'd best get over to Judge's now and be home before Dad comes back from across the Bay. He'll be watching every breath I take forever after. I'll see you tonight.'

I clambered back into the skiff, retying the blue ribbons under my chin. I clucked to Obie, who stuck his muzzle down through the floor of the duck blind, but stayed put.

'Come on,' I said impatiently. But he just hunkered down there and looked at me. Then it struck me. Of course I should leave him with Tunes. I'd worry less about her disappearing while I was gone, and she'd have some company. Obie often was out prowling overnight or for a couple of days before Dad got too riled about where he'd gone.

'Okay,' I said. 'You take good care of Tunes, hear?' Tunes lowered her head beside Obie's through the hole in the floor.

'Take him with you, Buck,' she said. 'I'm fine out here. With Obie, there's more chance of somebody seeing us. And what if Jumbo sees him?'

But Obie wouldn't budge. When Tunes tried to push him down into the skiff, he backed up and sat down.

'You make sure Jumbo doesn't hurt him. I got to get on up to Judge's,' I said. 'I'll feel easier knowing Obie's here. Don't you go taking any fool chances.' She squinted at me and looked as if she had something scornful to say. But she just waved.

On the way down Jumbo's creek and into the Bay, as I again did my best to impersonate Gran, the streamers on her hat blowing out behind me, the thing that had been tickling the back of my mind came forward. It wasn't really like Tunes to just set there, waiting on me to come along and find her.

I reckoned I'd been gone from home less than an hour, which meant I'd have plenty of time to talk to Judge if he was at home. I turned out toward the heart of the Bay, then headed down toward Church Creek, where Judge lived. The streamers of Gran's hat caught up with me and floated out around my face, the wind competing with the airstream from our forward progress.

The sky loomed all friendly and gentle, with gold-edged white clouds in playful animal shapes against the bright blue sky. Those days storms had got to be a habit, and I was mindful that a pretty sky like that was like as not to turn on me when I least expected it.

I felt so alone. As long as I could remember, Dad and Kneebone had known all the answers to anything that troubled Tunes and me. I tried to call up Gran's words about people's having good intentions and not letting their failings break my heart.

Outside the mouth of the creek, the Bay lay open and bottle-green, the sides of the gentle swells glassy before me.

I cut the engine and just sat there a bit, drifting and thinking. I always admired Tunes' mystery. Admired it, that is, when she wasn't using it against me. When she was, it made me hopping mad.

The sun was high and hot, turning my forearms and knees, which stuck out from under Gran's coverall, shiny and red.

About fifty feet out, a porpoise broke the surface of the water, followed by another and another, and still a fourth and a fifth, lazily making their way up the Bay in slow-motion arcs, searching out a school of menhaden.

It was all I could do to keep from jumping overboard and swimming toward them. But the last thing I needed was to have Dad suspecting I'd been out on the water, which he'd know for sure if I came home wet. So I just sat there, fairly twitching with excitement and wanting to be with them.

One day the summer before, Tunes and I had been lolling about on just such an afternoon, Tunes dangling her legs over the gunwales and me near-asleep in the stern. A school of porpoises came cavorting by, the sun shining silver from the curves of their sleek backs, just like these. I felt the boat skid sidewise lightly, and heard not a splash but a gentle pop as Tunes broke the surface of the water, diving over the side to swim toward them.

Her head came up about halfway between the boat and where those shiny grey little whales would be in about half a minute. She swam without a sound towards the place where they'd meet if neither changed course, the sun glittering off the water that clung to her arms mid-stroke and a wake fanning out behind her. She looked almost like one of those peaceable water creatures.

I'd joined her then, and the porpoises turned as one and swam toward us to investigate, as if some silent impulse linked their brains. And then they dived one by one in perfect formation like ballet dancers, each coming up to glide its body next to hers or mine, rubbing skin against skin from our knees to our shoulders.

Swimming with them was like being caught in a place without time, a moment I've thought on several occasions since might turn out to be one of the finest of my life. And then without a sound they were gone as suddenly as they'd appeared, leaving us the happier for having felt their slick, rubbery hides on ours.

Chapter 13

I turned the skiff then and set it at full throttle into Church Creek.

The water there was flat but rippled, and the skiff made hard little washboard slaps that you could hear rather than feel as it skidded around and into the tidal wash just inside the mouth of the creek.

Judge sat out on his dock, his rickety chair tipped back, with a fishing line in the water and a small blue plastic bucket of silversides next to his feet. His teeth were clamped on an old unlit pipe that was gnarled as his hands.

He saw me coming at a clip up the creek. He stood, took the pipe from his mouth, and put his hands on his hips. The khaki fishing hat sat at an impossible angle on the back of his head. He watched me manoeuvre up the current and land expertly at the back of his dock's crosspiece, where the lopsided wooden ladder hung in the water, its bottom rungs green with slime and pocked white with barnacles.

'Well now,' he said, serious but warm, tucking his pipe into the pocket of his faded blue work shirt. He was always glad to see me. 'What brings you out this fine day? I like your dress,' he added.

I snatched the hat off my head and untied Gran's coverall, tossing them both onto the floor of the skiff.

He took the painter and secured it to the piling, then gave me a hand up the last part of the ladder, which groaned and pivoted, even under my slight weight.

'Tunes and I need your help,' I said. He turned his face up toward the house, a big old brick place with dark green wooden shutters and a fine garden, as if to see whether Mrs Wickham was watching. I didn't know whether he saw her, but he bent quickly and picked up his fishing pole, reeled in the line, and tucked the bait bucket into the shade under the chair.

He looked rested and suntanned and fit and fully alert, for which I was grateful.

'Let's go out around the bend a bit, shall we?' he said, and we scrambled back down into the skiff. Judge pushed us out into the current, and we drifted back toward the Bay for a minute before I restarted the engine. We headed up into the cove behind Judge's farm, where there was plenty of tree shelter and a shoal bottom that meant nobody'd be poking around up in there and we'd have a private place to talk.

'What's all this about?' Judge asked. 'Your daddy'll skin you if he catches you out here with that skiff. Isn't a body on this neck doesn't know it, and I dare say there's a few who'd make it their business to let him know if they see you.'

'Yessir,' I said, impatient but mindful that I had to listen to his concern. 'But Tunes and me need your advice. Somehow – '

'Now, hold on, Buck. Where's Tunes, and when'd you talk to her?'

'Begging your pardon, Judge, I got precious little time before I have to get back.' I remembered Tunes' warning. But I decided if we were going to trust Judge, we were going to trust him. In for a penny, in for a pound, Gran always said. I took a deep breath. 'I promised her I wouldn't tell, but I think I can get her to come back with me. Please, please don't tell anybody anything about this.'

'Okay, Buck. Client privilege.' He nodded for me to go on.

'Mr Rawlin's done some terrible bad things by my reckoning. I'm sure he killed Jorge. We need to figure out just how we can prove Jumbo did it so's Sheriff doesn't arrest Tunes.'

'You're right sure it was Mr Rawlin.' It was not a question. Judge's bright blue eyes were fastened on me like a dog eyeing its dinner. I nodded my head emphatically.

I told him briefly about seeing Jumbo the morning we found Jorge and the lies he'd told Sheriff about seeing Tunes and Jorge together, their romance and all.

'Jorge had more sense than that,' Judge said. 'But somebody had a motive. You got a body. If you can find a motive – well, you might just be able to convince Sheriff Tunes didn't do any killing. You have any idea why Jumbo might have done it?'

'I don't know exactly why, sir, though Mr Rawlin didn't like Jorge askin' for repairs on the labour housing out on the county road. And I recall Dad saying they had words another time when Jorge asked for a van to take the women from the camp grocery-shopping once a week.'

'That's not quite a motive kind of thing,' Judge said. 'I'm thinking more about something that would've raised Jumbo Rawlin's dander.'

An image gnawed at the back of my mind. The way Tunes bolted when we found the body, her saying she meant to leave the Shore. I sat still, thinking hard. 'Now you mention it, Tunes might have an idea. What Jumbo told Sheriff doesn't make sense any which way. When I found the body, she was so afraid she'd get blamed she bolted. Maybe there was another reason – like maybe she knew something she didn't want to tell. I don't have any idea what it would be, or even that she'd tell me now. But I can ask her.'

'You best tell her a lot rides on her sharing that information with you. Like whether she goes free. And maybe even whether you go free.'

'I didn't have anything to do – '

'Well now, neither did Tunes have anything to do with Jorge's murder, did she? If you're setting out to prove that, you'd best be thinking that way. Mr Rawlin's very clever – not to mention devious – and I dare say *he* doesn't mean to take any blame. If I were Tunes, I wouldn't expect Sheriff to cut her any slack. Not unless she comes forward and tells what she knows about it, anyway.'

'Judge,' I said, wanting to get to something more concrete, 'what about the gun they found? They say it's Tunes' – someone found it in Little Creek and turned it over to Sheriff. I don't know how Mr Rawlin got Tunes' gun, but if he did use it to kill Jorge, why would he hide it? Wouldn't he want it to be found so's she'd get blamed?'

'Why, I don't rightly know,' said Judge, scratching the white stubble on his broad chin. 'Seems to me a murderer who used someone else's gun might leave it somewheres he was pretty sure it'd be found, like in shoal water where crabbers are working. But you'd best leave gun business to Sheriff. What you have to do – and it's something I believe you *can* do – is find out about a motive. Sheriff's a reasonable man. If you can show him reasonable doubt about what he thinks Tunes' motive was – a romance gone bad – you might have a case.'

I took a deep breath. It was the first shred of hope yet that we might be able to clear Tunes. I didn't know whether I could produce a motive, but I was beginning to get a strong feeling that Tunes knew a lot she wasn't saying.

'Yessir,' I said. But now I was faced with something I'd never had much luck with: getting Tunes to talk when she'd decided not to.

'And, Buck, don't forget,' said Judge. 'If Tunes will agree to it, you can bring her here and we'll go to Sheriff together. I'm sure he'll listen to her. You and Tunes watch your step. Hear?' He stuck out his hand and we shook on it.

I thanked him. He gave me a good man-sized hug.

'I got to get back,' I said, and returned him to his dock. He climbed up the ladder as nimble as a young man. Halfway down the creek, I turned back to see him as he'd been when I'd headed up toward his dock, tipped back on his chair, line in the water, bait bucket at his feet.

I ran the skiff aground just where Dad had tethered it to the tree before and snapped the new lock onto the chain. I hightailed it on up to the barn, where I hung Gran's coverall and hat on the hook by the door where I'd found them, then up to the house. All in all, I'd been gone less than two hours.

Kneebone was out in Gran's herb garden behind the kitchen, his hands in the back pockets of his jeans, stretching down his suspenders. The sun shone bright on the nut-brown skin of his balding head. When he saw me round the turn in the path, he let his hands drop down to his sides, turned on the heel of his heavy work boot, and headed off toward the driveway, where his old green truck sat waiting for him like a lazy beetle.

I wanted with all my heart to run to him and tell him I'd found Tunes and that she was just fine. I wanted to comfort him, tell him Judge and me would make it all right for Tunes. I wanted to take comfort myself in his strong silence, see one of his rare, perfect smiles when he found out she was fine.

Just like Kneebone to make sure I was okay and then leave me be. I was sure he'd heard me roar up the back-side of the creek in the skiff, and I knew he'd wonder if I'd seen Tunes. But he'd never ask if I didn't tell him, and I knew he wouldn't tell Dad.

Kneebone sat by the end of the driveway waiting for Dad and Gran and Mama to show. He was keeping his word to Dad, after a fashion, that he'd keep an eye out for me.

I swallowed to prevent the pain in my throat from prompting tears for love of him and for wanting to trust him the way I always had. But he was trying to keep Tunes and me apart, just like Dad was, and I wasn't up to taking a chance on their interfering, calling Sheriff or the Reverend, until Tunes and me'd had a chance to get ourselves out of this mess.

I hated to admit it, but I hadn't forgiven either Kneebone or Dad, and there was an element of enjoying their discomfort while I proved them wrong. I think I took some strength from that, and it bolstered my determination to stand by Tunes and show she was innocent.

I got my weeding basket and digger and was just making my way through the row of box hedge nearest the house, slapping at the first of the season's deerflies, when Dad pulled in to the drive and Kneebone pulled out.

That evening, after I finished the dishes, I took myself down to sit at the edge of the creek on Granddaddy's old wooden dock chair, which I turned around to face back up toward the house. The evening was long and lonely without Obie, and the days had been so empty without Tunes, it was like I never was able to unload my troubles and my thoughts, so they weighed heavy on me.

And not being able to look forward to going out later with a spotlight to net bait in the shallows of the creek made the time pass unnaturally slow.

Fireflies winked here and there like so many fairies, up the stretch of grass from where I sat at the shore end of the dock clear up to the rose hedge in Gran's garden. It didn't cheer me any – if anything, it made the evening seem sadder and lonelier.

The more I thought on it, the more anxious I was to get out to see Tunes again that night. There was something not quite setting right with me about Tunes and how she was hunkered down out there all purposeful-like.

Tunes was not the waiting kind – most especially not the kind waiting on someone to rescue her. I was afraid what she was holding back on telling was something that would endanger her, and I wasn't at all certain I could persuade her to tell me, let alone tell Sheriff.

Chapter 14

The night was warm and still, and the mosquitoes were buzzing, the bullfrogs and peepers were singing their night songs, and the stars lit up the sky and water like diamonds set in black glass. It was a night to make your heart sing.

Mama and Dad and Gran all went to their rooms early, which was a family tradition once it got warm every year and the planting was well under way and we were all bone-tired. Mama ran a cool bath for me in the white porcelain tub in the bathroom beside my bedroom. Then she said good night and went in to read.

I lay in the cool water, immersed to my chin with my eyes closed, feeling the heat leave my body. Someone tapped lightly on the door.

'Who is it?' I asked.

'May I come in?' It was Dad.

'Yessir,' I said. My heart took a leap. It occurred to me that he'd found out I'd had the skiff out.

He pulled a wicker stool up beside the old footed bath-tub. I felt a surge of hope then that maybe he'd tell me he'd changed his mind about Tunes.

'I know a lot of things don't make sense to you, Buck,' he said. He looked right uncomfortable.

'Yessir,' I said, not wanting much to help him out, or to act hopeful.

'It might appear to you I'm taking Mr Rawlin's side over Tunes'.'

'Yessir,' I said again.

'It's not that at all. I want you to hear me out. You don't have to agree with me. I don't like the two of us walking around not talking to each other.'

I lay in the water, listening. He told me all the reasons why Sheriff thought it was Tunes had killed Jorge and not Jumbo, and why it all added up. It was no more than I already knew, turned back to front by Sheriff's interpretation.

'Sometimes it's hard to face facts, because they can undo a lot of what you always believed in,' Dad said when I tried to protest.

I realized he was just trying to win me over to his way of thinking, and it made me angry all over again. Still, I kept in mind Gran's words about forgiveness.

'I thought a lot about it, Dad,' I said. 'And I keep coming back to this: you don't trust me because I lied about Tunes being with me that day. But I lied to protect her, because I didn't trust Sheriff not to blame her. And now I don't trust you for the same reason. You and me have good reason not to trust each other.'

'Buck . . .' But whatever other words he had to say were temporarily stuck inside him.

Having someone you loved expect you to agree to something that wasn't right felt very bad, and somehow very grownup. Without letting him finish what he had to say, I sank slowly below the surface of the water. While I was down there I thought about what Dad had said about evil – that I might be mistaking roughness and gracelessness for it in Jumbo – and how the truth could rearrange what you believed in. A small ring of pain constricted my throat. I stayed underwater until my lungs begged for air.

When I came up again, he was still sitting there, looking at me like he'd lost me. I gulped down another breath and resubmerged. I looked up through the water and caught a wavery image of him standing up to leave.

I went to bed right after, skin still damp, on clean cool sheets, the warm cross-breeze blowing the curtains into the dark away from the screened windows, and an old long-blade fan whirring softly overhead.

Despite the pain I felt righteous, and it renewed my determination to make things right for Tunes.

The May night air, soft and damp and warm, and the swamp grass smells wafted in with the lace curtains and the songs of the night creatures. Every once in a while a big lunker made a hollow splash down on the creek. I forgot my sorrow long enough to wonder if it was an otter diving off the bank, or a drum whipping its tail, or a bluefish wild with hunger for some little fingerling. Then the ache in my heart returned, and I thought if this was what growing up felt like, I didn't want any part of it.

I fell into a deep sleep and awoke some hours later, well past midnight, with a swish of wet against my face and arm as a rain-dampened lace curtain blew across me. The wind howled and set the windows to rattling in their sashes. The rain was just beginning. Branches clattered against the house and over the roof. I'd barely closed the window when the rain hissed and spat against the panes. Loud rumbles of thunder followed the lightning in shortening intervals as the centre of the storm drew closer.

The door to Mama and Dad's bedroom was open, and their snores'd like to scare off a ghost on a quiet night. That night it was a mere ruffling sound in comparison to the storm outside. I put on my boots and ran down the stairs, mindful that the clatter of the wind and rain would cover any noise I might have made.

I wasn't hungry, but I hadn't eaten much supper and knew I'd need something to keep going on. I quickly made myself a peanut butter sandwich, wiped off the knife and returned it to the drawer, took a long swig straight from the milk jug, then tiptoed back upstairs to fix my pillows so it looked like I was still in bed. In the kitchen again, I took a green plastic garbage bag from the pantry.

I got two sets of foul-weather gear from the back hall closet, pulled on one slicker, overalls and boots, and stuffed the other set into the plastic bag for Tunes.

Then I slipped out the kitchen door, pulling it to with a faint whoosh of air. I noted that the main part of the storm had stayed out on the Bay, and was moving farther on up north.

The wind had not begun to die down yet, but if the storm kept moving through I probably could make it out to the duck blind. I reckoned Tunes would be more likely to come in with me on a bad-weather night. Sheriff wasn't likely to be out looking for her, and the skiff should be able to deal with the wind. It'd be an uncomfortable ride over to Judge's, but not dangerous.

Down the other side of the garden on the path to the inlet a barn owl let out a high hissy whistle, calling to its fledglings in the storm.

I didn't need the flashlight. The storm flashed pink and blue over the horizon, and the intervals between thunderclaps grew longer.

The skiff was where I'd left it, bucking against the chain locked to the trunk of a tree on the bank. I snapped open the lock and reached under the seats for the oars. Even with the storm I was afraid someone'd hear the motor. I hadn't rowed in the two years before, and at first the oars rolled wildly in the oarlocks. Finally the pull of the water steadied against my hands.

The oarlocks groaned as I hauled against the waves and turned the bow into the creek. Once out in the stream, I started the motor and the outgoing tide bore me along like a feather.

It wasn't until I was out on the Bay, battling the swells, the wind tearing the breath right out of my mouth, blinded by the rain, that it struck me. Something Tunes and I'd been talking about in another context: Jumbo walked around with his .22 rifle like it was attached to his arm. We had said that to each other many times after Kneebone's hound went missing, then turned up with a .22 hole through his head.

What I hadn't thought about before was this: that old hound dog'd been shot with a .22, which was what made us think Jumbo'd done it. Most folks on the Shore used shotguns. And the dog's head was stove in – just like Jorge's had been. No way a .22 bullet would do that. Suddenly my mind's eye captured an image of someone beating the hound dog – perhaps someone in a fit of rage, or fear – and then shooting it. And then the image of the same thing happening to Jorge took my breath away like someone'd kicked me swiftly in the gut. Both the same. If there'd been any doubt in my mind before that moment that Jumbo'd killed Jorge, there was none after.

By the time I got out to the duck blind, the wind had died down a fair bit. The chop had been severe on the way out, but I made slow headway, taking care to cut directly into the waves. The skiff bucked like an ornery horse, slapping down into the trough of each wave with an ominous groan.

The rain still drove sideways and bit into my face, so's it stung to keep my eyes open. My foul-weather gear shone a ghosty greenish yellow in the flickers and flashes of the storm. I cut the motor before I got offshore of Jumbo's and put the oars back in the oarlocks.

I didn't see the duck blind until I was almost under it. Just as I rowed the last few feet, straining my eyes to see, a great flash of lightning lit the creek and woods and everything within view in a weird two-dimensional picture. The blind had held together just fine through the storm. The reeds that hid it and made it look like just another little marshy tump still clung to the outer walls.

Inside, it looked tight and cosy as ever. I switched on Dad's six-volt flashlight. Tunes and Obie lay curled up on the floor, back to back, dead asleep. The light wool blanket I'd brought covered them both. Tunes' hands were crossed at the wrists in front of her face. Her head rested on a pillow she'd made of the denim jacket wrapped around her shoes. The storm must have had them up most of the night, because they didn't hear me or see the light, and I couldn't hear or see them breathe.

'Tunes!' I said. 'Get up!'

I shined the light directly on Tunes' face. She lay still a moment with one eye open a little crack. Obie's tail whumped the floor once, heavily. Obie gave new meaning to the term 'dog-tired'. When he was spent, you could pick him up by the feet and drag him without waking him.

Tunes sat up, rubbing her eyes. Obie still didn't stir. I dropped the foul-weather gear on the floor.

'We'd best get going while the storm is still playing around here,' I said. Tunes rummaged through one of the bags I'd brought.

'What difference does it make?' she asked, her words sharp-edged with an impatience I didn't understand. She found something and it clattered as she laid it on the low wooden stand she used for a table. She fished around again for a moment, then lit a match. In its flare she held up a candle. She lit it and tipped it, watching as a molten puddle of wax formed on the table. She set the candle upright in it and leaned back on her heels.

'We won't be so likely to be seen or heard if we go on the storm,' I said.

'And just where do you think we're going?' she asked, narrowing her eyes at me over the candle.

132

'Tunes, the only chance you got is to go in. Judge says Sheriff will listen to you. We can show him reasonable-like that what Jumbo said about you and Jorge isn't true.' I told her what I'd thought of, about the hound's head being stove in just like Jorge's.

'Sheriff'll see that what we say makes sense. Once he hears your side of things, he'll know he has no case against you, and maybe has one against Jumbo.'

She sat silent for a full couple of minutes. She rocked back on her heels, thinking. I didn't interrupt her.

'You believe in evil, Buck?' she asked then.

She'd caught me off my guard. I'd been thinking a lot lately about evil – such as, maybe it was more than just the opposite of good. After reflecting on what'd happened to Jorge I'd begun to think the Baptists might be right. Dewey Morgan's mama was a Baptist, and she believed evil's a powerful force that stalks the earth.

'I don't know,' I said. 'I used to think there was a logical explanation for things that happened. Like maybe Jumbo'd killed Jorge not on purpose but by accident, in a fit of temper. Maybe the fit of temper's what's evil. But then maybe Jumbo's crazy, and that's the evil . . . And the fact Jumbo'd try to blame you for killin' Jorge and didn't waste a second being sorry . . . '

My thoughts were all disjointed, as I'd never tested them by saying them out loud.

'I expect you gotta feel evil's power to know what it is,' Tunes said, her voice real quiet. 'The reasons some things happen don't matter. Evil's evil, and the more powerful the evil is, the quicker you gotta do it in – kill it – before it up 'n' kills you!'

'Don't talk crazy, Tunes,' I said, trying not to let the panic I felt into my voice. 'You kill Jumbo and what'll that get you but sent away? That's no answer.'

'Well, you think I'm gonna convince Sheriff I didn't kill Jorge? Sheriff's like most white folks who think they've known all their lives how niggers behave.'

That word again. It made me wince.

'He *wants* to believe Jorge 'n' me slipped off together every chance we got. 'Fore you convince him that's not true, you have to rearrange his whole view of the world!'

Ugly as those words were, I knew she had reason to believe them. I didn't have a clue how some folks' minds could think something all their lives, with plenty of evidence around to show them wrong. I always thought there was something in their eyes kept them from seeing, but I could never put my finger on what it was.

'But killing a person, Tunes, I don't care how evil you think Jumbo is – *that's* evil.'

'You want to know something, Buck? There's a lot more evil things than killing a man.'

Her talk – both the words and tone of voice – scared me, and I growled a little, sounding more belligerent than I felt.

'Yeah?' I said. 'Like what?'

'Like Jumbo puttin' his hands on a girl, places a man's hands shouldn't oughtta be.'

Tunes' voice had gone real quiet. I wanted to stop her from telling me. I didn't want to know this.

'Like pushin' her down on the ground and laughing like it's a game, him wanting to put his big wet mouth all over her,' she went on. 'Like telling her after, he'd whup her bloody and burn her daddy's house if she dared tell anybody what he'd done to her.'

Her voice had been ominous with quiet and calm, but now it shook with hurt and rage. 'I was eleven years old, Buck! I was too scared to do anything! I don't know now whether I'll ever be right!' A great sob tore itself from her, and she bent her head in the stillness of the candle's glow.

I sat immobile as a stone, afraid to move, afraid to wake myself out of this nightmare, for surely this was one. I felt revulsion first, then shame at the revulsion, and then a great wave of sorrow washed over me, and I felt as if I might drown in a wide sea of hopelessness. My own selfish sense of loss was unbearable. I shivered and my face was wet with tears.

'Didn't you tell Kneebone? You been carrying this on you all alone, Tunes?'

A strange cry bubbled up and caught in my throat, and I put my arms around her shoulders and held on to her. We clung to each other and we cried for just a minute or so, with great racking sobs, before Tunes pulled away. It felt strange, holding her like that, and I felt uncomfortable, glad she moved first.

She leaned back and sat with her spine against the wall and dried her face with the tail of her worn flannel shirt.

'I didn't tell Kneebone 'cuz I knew he'd go right over there and kill Jumbo. You know he would've spent the rest of his life in jail. If they didn't put him in the 'lectric chair. I need him too much to have that happen. Since he didn't know, Jumbo kept coming after me.

'And I couldn't tell you. I felt ashamed, so powerful ashamed, like it was all my fault. Jumbo kept telling me I was asking for it. I began to wonder if he was right. I couldn't tell anybody.'

She wasn't crying any more, but her words came out dry and harsh between little hiccups. She rubbed her nose with the heel of her hand.

'Now I manage to stay away from him pretty much. But sometimes he comes lookin' for me.' Her voice went up in a little squeak at the end.

'Wasn't there some way to stop him?' As soon as the words were out I wished I could swallow them back up. They sounded first like an accusation that I didn't really mean, and second like a justification of what she had in her mind, to kill Jumbo.

She watched me for a long moment through the candlelight.

'He said he'd get the land under our house from your daddy someday.' I started to protest, but she rushed on.

'I've seen Jumbo take folks' land, Buck, ten acres here, twenty there. And Lord save my soul, I believed him. He said if I "cooperated" – that's the word he used – Kneebone and I could stay on. If I didn't, he'd burn down our house. And don't think there's not plenty of black women on the Shore who've had that exact thing happen to them. And I'm not talking about a hundred years ago, neither.'

I swallowed hard. I thought of all the times Tunes talked about leaving that house, tossing it off with a shrug of one shoulder, when I knew how much she loved that place where her mama had died when she was just a baby, where she and Kneebone tended their garden, coaxing tomatoes and peppers and squash and okra from the oak-acid, sandy soil.

Pictures of Tunes flitted through my memory: Tunes a slopy-eyed little girl with chestnut skin in a flouncy pink dress at her sixth birthday party; Tunes in a bathing suit that was too big, handed down as it was from Mazie's daughters; Tunes at ten, her legs so long and skinny Kneebone and I used to call her 'Grandmammy Longlegs'; Tunes slipping off for days at a time. I'd ask Kneebone where she'd gone.

One time he sighed and shrugged and said to me, 'Girl doesn't answer me, I ask where she goes. It's like she got a angel in her that takes her away. But he delivers her back safe again, so I don't ask any more and I'm thankful.'

'The week before we found Jorge,' Tunes said, 'Jumbo came after me again. I barely managed to get away from him and out into the woods. I knew I had to do something.' She rubbed the ball of one foot over the instep of the other and stared down at them as if they belonged to somebody else.

'So that Friday I went looking for him with my gun. I was going to kill him.' Her tone was flat and lifeless.

'I went down to the woods near the road that leads to Jumbo's property. At first I'd planned to hide up in a tree and shoot him as he drove down that dirt road.

'I walked halfway down the lane and climbed up into one of those big old dogwoods and sat there waiting for him to come along. The more I waited, the more I thought if I killed him I'd probably spend the rest of my life in jail. And he sure enough isn't worth that.

'I've thought a thousand times since, if I'd 'a done him in, Jorge might be alive today,' she said. She cried again, then wiped her eyes on her shirttail, and blew her nose.

'Anyway, I decided to warn Jumbo. Give him something to think on that would make him reconsider before coming after me another time. I climbed down from the tree and stood by the side of his road in the bushes. When I saw him coming, I stepped out in front of his truck. I was holding the gun up and down behind my back so's he couldn't see I had it.

'He stopped and stared for a second. He said to me, "When I want you I'll come get you." So I told him if he ever came to get me again I'd kill him and burn *his* house down. He laughed. I raised up my gun, and you should have seen the look on his face. I blew out the windshield. I think the bullet hit the gun rack where he carries his .22 behind him in the cab of the truck. He went to grab the gun and it was stuck.

'Those few seconds he struggled with his gun were sure 'n' true lucky for me – gave me a chance to hightail it on out of there. Jumbo never came looking at the house for me. But I guessed he wouldn't. I figure deep down underneath, evil's a coward . . .'

Chapter 15

If my mind had snapped to like a policeman's the day we'd found Jorge, it reverted to near-criminal sharpness after Tunes told me about what Jumbo'd done to her. I had to think of the most convincing argument to get her to come with me.

'I been thinking it's up to us to prove Jumbo killed Jorge,' I said. 'He's counting on your running away. Going to Sheriff is the only way to clear your name, and if we don't, he's going to get away with it.'

'And what's Sheriff going to believe?' she said, defiance shaking in her voice. 'If he found my gun and came direct to arrest me, why would he change his mind now? Nothing's changed, Buck.'

I took a deep breath.

'I was hoping you could tell me why Sheriff should change his mind. Judge says we need to tell Sheriff what Jumbo's motive was.'

'You planning on knocking on Jumbo's door, Buck? Sayin', " 'Scuse me, Mr Rawlin, but would you please tell us why you killed Jorge so my friend Tunes here doesn't get blamed?" ' She had that osprey look to her eyes again, and that old devil scorn had crept back into her voice.

'Don't be smart-alecky,' I said. 'How'd Jumbo get your gun anyways?'

Tunes sucked in her breath, and something about the way she moved reminded me of how she looked two seconds before she jumped over the side of the skiff the day we'd found Jorge's body. I understood right then and there that she knew very well what'd happened, and had all along.

The storm must have stopped moving and settled in. The wind and rain still whipped around outside something fierce.

'Judge says you and me both could go to jail if you don't tell what-all you know,' I said. 'Says Jumbo's smart enough to see he doesn't take any blame, and that leaves you. And me.'

'Hah!' she said with a snort. 'No way you'd get blamed. Sheriff knows you're an innocent little kid who's too worshipful of some bad black girl!'

I paused. I knew I had to mean this with all my heart, because there was no fooling her.

'Tunes, if you don't promise to come with me and tell Sheriff exactly what happened, I'm going to go in and tell him myself. Right now.'

'What makes you think I'd know exactly what happened, Buck Smith?'

''Cuz I can tell by the look of you, that's how. You look like you might jump clear out of your skin and leave it in a pile behind you. You've already told me what Jumbo did to you. Why can't you tell me why he killed Jorge?'

She was dead silent, her eyes moving quickly around the blind. She looked like a wild animal, cornered and not knowing which way to escape.

'Were you there when it happened?' She didn't answer, just kept cutting her eyes around the duck blind. 'Tunes? Were you?' She was quiet for a full minute, but I waited her out because I knew she was going to tell me.

'No, not when it happened. I told you I ran away while Jumbo was trying to get his gun out of the rack. Well, he gave up right quick and ran after me into the woods. He caught up a couple hundred feet from the road. He hit me with the flat of his hand. I fell and dropped my gun. It lay there on the ground in the woods, and I haven't seen it since. I went back to look for it, but it was gone.'

'What happened then?' I asked.

'Jumbo grabbed ahold of my hair and yanked me up from the ground. He kept slapping me, and all the time he had my hair tight in his fist. He'd slap me until I fell down, then haul me up by the hair and slap me down again.'

My blood began to churn in my veins. I could hear it hissing through my head, and at that moment I wanted to kill Jumbo, too. I sat still, clenching and reclenching my fists until my wrists ached.

'Jumbo'd hit me before. He was always careful not to leave any cuts or bruises. That day he slapped me so hard it made my teeth slam together.

'I heard a truck turn down the road and I hollered. It was Jorge coming to talk to Jumbo about something. The work crew, most likely. They were about to start planting at Jumbo's place. Jorge must have heard me, because he came running down the path, right toward where we were.

'My nose was bleeding and my eyes were streaming. Jumbo hit me hard then in the stomach, knocked the breath clear out of me. Then he grabbed me up and tried to haul me away. I was struggling hard to get my breath back. He held me pinned against his hip with one arm, and he clamped his other hand over my mouth. I kept kicking at him and catching ahold of the trunks of the loblollies. I was afraid he'd kill me, sure as anything. He'd take his hand away from my mouth to grab my arms down from the trees, and I'd try to holler again. I was like a one-person three-ring circus.

'Jorge followed us. It wasn't hard for him to catch up, with me grabbing on to the tree trunks, and every couple of times I'd get my hands free I'd pull Jumbo's hat down over his eyes and he'd have to pull it back and I'd grab on to another tree.'

She laughed at the image of it, and I laughed, too, till she stopped all of a sudden and buried her face in her hands. Her shoulders lifted and fell. Then she dropped her hands with a loud sigh. Her eyes were dry. The wind died a bit, and Tunes' face had an eerie glow in the yellow light of the candle.

'Jorge was so brave and calm, Buck. His voice and eyes were so steady. Asked why was I crying and why Jumbo had ahold of me. Jumbo said he'd caught me stealing. Jorge looked at me to see what I was going to say. I still hadn't caught my breath and couldn't get a word out. Jorge knew it was a lie.

' "Let her go", Jorge said. And Jumbo went, "You mind your own business." Jorge just started to walk toward us, and Jumbo must have been distracted, because I managed to get myself loose of him.

'Jorge told me to go on home. But I couldn't make my legs move. It was like they'd put roots down right there where I stood, like I was one of those big old loblolly pines.

'He said to Jumbo, "How long you think you can get away with abusing people?" And Jumbo told him to mind his own business again. Started walking back up toward his truck. Jorge shouted at me to get out of there fast and not come back. So I turned tail and ran all the way back home.'

'Did Jumbo have his gun?' I asked.

'It was still in his gun rack. But my gun was there, lying on the ground where I'd dropped it. Don't you see? He used my gun to kill Jorge and then threw it in the creek.' She was quiet for a moment. 'Funny thing is I never heard a shot.'

'He bashed Jorge's head in first,' I said. 'Shot him later.'

Tunes shook her head. She leaned forward and put her hands on the table, and knelt that way, her arms out stiff in front of her. I was conscious of the distance between us, and I felt guilty, confused, and ashamed for letting what'd happened to her make me feel so uncomfortable.

I was thinking back to the day we'd found Jorge. There was no sign of the struggle she described. Her hands were all scuffed and her fingernails were dirty – but she'd been digging up roots with her bare hands and then hauling them out of the garden, and I didn't think anything of it. But she'd been in a good mood – until we found Jorge's body, that is.

'Judge is wrong. Sheriff's not going to believe me all of a sudden,' she said. 'Even if I tell him what we just put together, he could still say I killed Jorge. It's Jumbo Rawlin's word against mine. And Jumbo's fixed up some pretty good lies.'

'We got to take a chance,' I said. And then I had a thought that was pure inspiration. 'If you don't try, Tunes, your name will never be cleared. And then where will you be? You going to hide out the rest of your life? You want folks thinking you did it and then ran away? You *got* to try!'

Tunes didn't even bother with her scornful look. Even without it I remembered how she'd told me, time and again, how the rules applied differently to her and Kneebone than they did to me and my family, and how I could never understand.

'Think, Tunes,' I said. 'Tell me everything that happened, even if it doesn't seem to be important. Did anybody see you?'

'I got to Jumbo's about four o'clock that afternoon, right after school. It was about a half hour later Jumbo came along, and just a few minutes after that, Jorge came.

'Later, about six, before Kneebone came home, I went on my bicycle looking for Jorge at his office over at the labour camp at Crook's Neck Farm. I wanted to be sure he was all right. Menendez was standing around like he always does, with his hands in his pockets, not saying anything. He's the only one saw me. He told me Jorge was supposed to be back at five. I never thought something like that would happen, Buck! When I saw you next day I was just sure he was all right, that we'd see him again around the farm, whistling like he always did, or down at the dock.'

She cried quietly then. I moved to sit closer beside her, not touching her. I wanted to lay my arm across her shoulders, but I couldn't make myself do it.

'It wasn't your fault, Tunes. None of this is your fault. It was Jumbo. You're right. He's some powerful kind of evil. I never knew anybody had it in them to do the kind of things he's done. But it's up to us to prove he did it. All we can do is tell Sheriff your story. Judge'll help us. We got to try!'

Obie butted his nose in between us, and Tunes petted him absently, then wiped at her tears with the flat of her hand.

The wind still blew at a clip outside, but it had died down from when I'd pulled the skiff in under the blind. The rain was lighter and swept over the snug little shelter in soft, whispery gusts.

I'd pulled myself up to be Tunes' equal for the first time. So much had happened so quickly, I felt like I'd grown up ten years' worth in that one night. I had appealed to her sense of justice, and it felt like the right thing to do. I felt strong, like I knew in my heart how right I was, and it didn't matter what anyone else thought – not even Sheriff. But I felt sure he'd believe us, and we'd prove him and Dad wrong.

Tunes sat back, and I handed her the foul-weather gear. She was shivering. She hauled on the pants, wriggled her shoulders into the suspenders, pulled the slicker over her head, and slid her feet into the boots.

By then the wind was dying way down. The rain still slid sideways in gusts, but there was not the ferocious wailing and the stinging of raindrops hurled like missiles. Obie leapt into the skiff after us and lay with his chin between his paws on the floorboards.

The lightning persisted, but it was farther away and clouded over, providing some dull light to see by as we made our way through the shallow water spiked with cordgrass toward the deeper channel.

Chapter 16

I struggled with the oars, which spun awkwardly in my hands again and skipped across the top of the water. I concentrated on getting coordinated, and was surprised when the boat skidded sideways.

I looked up in time to see the yellow stripes of reflective tape on the sleeves of Tunes' slicker waver a few feet off in the retreating lightning.

'Tunes!' I shouted. It was the second time she'd bolted like that, and this time I knew I had to get her back. 'Get her, Obie,' I shouted. 'Hold on to her.' Obie leapt over the gunwales and chased after her. I don't know what he thought, maybe that this was a game, but he sure looked like he didn't mean to let her get away. It gave me a moment to grab up the painter and haul the skiff along behind me until I could lodge it on a tump of cord-grass.

Obie caught up with Tunes and tackled her from behind, grabbing her boot in his jaws. She tripped in the shallow water and sprawled. Obie lost his grip for a second, but caught her again by the heel and held on.

Tunes kicked at him, but he managed to keep her down until I caught up. I hauled on her arm, and she struggled to her feet.

'Where do you think you're going?' I shouted. 'You can't hide from us, Tunes. We'd find you anywheres on the Eastern Shore. I know I'm right, and you just got to trust me. Now get back in the skiff. We're going in to Judge's.'

She turned as if she meant to come along, but then snatched her arm away and surged through the shoal water toward shore.

The ghostly pink and blue pulses of the retreating storm lit Jumbo's house, which loomed above us like something from a Frankenstein movie. Once Tunes hit land, she jumped up and hauled down a hanging pine branch. I dodged around it, and scrambled up the bank behind her.

All along the slope down to the water the pine trees creaked and groaned and whistled in the wind. I hoped they made enough of a din so that Jumbo couldn't hear whatever noise we made.

I had trouble staying up with her, but I kept on until we hit more level ground, still in the cover of the pine trees. I heard the rustle of oilskin as she shucked off her slicker and rain pants.

I removed my gear, too, and then it was easier to run, crouched into the wind. We were halfway to Jumbo's house from the waterfront when a loud crack followed by a thump sent me lurching face first into the glop of pine needles and mud several feet behind Tunes. She fell flat on her stomach, hitting the ground head up. I shinnied up beside her, grabbed her ankle, and held on.

'Let me go, Buck,' she said. She was crying, and I half sensed she wasn't really sure of what she was doing. But her voice was loud, and I was worried Jumbo might hear us.

'Hush!' I said. 'Don't you know where we are?'

'Please,' Tunes said. 'I got to leave. Sheriff won't ever believe me. I'll go to jail and Kneebone'll be shamed.'

'Not as bad as if you run away,' I said. I wiped the grainy mud from my face and tried not to clench my teeth, which gritted loud and sickening inside my head. I was trying to decide whether the crack we'd heard was a branch falling or a rifle shot.

Tunes raised her head slightly and looked back. I still had hold of her ankle, but somehow she slipped my grip and was gone, silent and darting like a hummingbird up the gentle slope in front of me.

Tunes was both faster and quieter than me, but I was desperate to catch up with her and persuade her to come back with me. I lay there a second and tried to see what direction she'd taken. Just then a muffled crunching sound came from what seemed just a few feet from my shoulder. The sound stopped and then I heard it again, and again, at slow, even intervals.

I realized with a chill of horror that the sounds were footsteps. Slowly I moved my right hand, which had been curled under my left shoulder. I wiped my fingers on my T-shirt, and cleared some mud from my eyes. The moan of the wind and creaking of the trees covered the soft sucking noises of the mud when I moved.

Not five yards away stood Jumbo, looking menacing as a stalking lion. He carried his gun in both hands across his chest, like he aimed to use it soon.

I lay in a small depression with a large fallen branch between him and me. He must have heard us and come down from the house through the woods. He was doubling back up the slope toward the house, where he had his eyes fixed on something. I looked in the direction of his gaze and saw the light from the pole beside the barn.

Jumbo never once looked toward me but was intent on the direction Tunes had taken. He set himself a steady course up the hill toward the side of the barn. I could see now his fancy truck sat behind it, just an inch or two of chrome bumper peeping out from the driveway, which ran between the house and the barn. I wondered where Obie'd got to.

My brain near clicked, I was trying so hard to think how I could let Tunes know Jumbo was stalking her. But I couldn't even see her for the way she moved, silent and invisible. I was terrified. Every fibre of my being twitched with wanting to get on out of there, but I knew I had to warn her, to get both of us away.

I waited until Jumbo's back was full toward me. I cursed the lightning, which had diminished to sporadic little shows of blue light that made keeping track of him difficult. It would have made his watching Tunes just as difficult, except that the pole light near the barn would throw her into a haloed silhouette once she came out in the open to cross the expanse of yard.

I could see Jumbo somewhat better once he, too, had moved between me and the golden pool of light up by the barn. It took every ounce of courage I could muster to pick myself up slowly from the ground. In that instant it was like a giant hand picked me up and set my feet lightly on the ground beneath me.

I stayed behind Jumbo, closing the distance between us. I had a little plan in my mind, but it went only so far as spoiling his aim when he raised the gun to shoot at her. I could not think beyond that.

Against the light the merest sliver of a shadow flitted. I almost thought I was mistaken, but my focused mind registered it was Tunes.

I timed it carefully. As Jumbo raised the gun to his shoulder, I hurled myself at the back of his knees. It felt like I was moving in slow motion, but my aim was true. Jumbo fired off-balance, and in that frozen splinter of a second I realized the crack we'd heard earlier down in the trees had been a gunshot muffled by the wind, and not a breaking branch, as I'd thought.

I scrambled wildly then to untangle myself from Jumbo's legs, and hollered in panic for Tunes. The seconds seemed to stretch into hours as I lashed out with my hands and feet, trying to keep Jumbo off his balance, all the while yelling with all that I had in my lungs. I couldn't see Jumbo's gun, and for a second I hoped that he'd dropped it. I realized by then I'd lost any advantage that Jumbo's surprise might have afforded me.

He stood and shook me off like a crumb. His gun was aimed at me. I knew he couldn't see me very well, and I looked around wildly. I dived and rolled to one side just as he pulled the trigger. My head rang with the report, and bits of pine needles and mud spat up from the earth and stung my face.

It took a second to realize I hadn't been hit. My hand closed over a punky piece of fallen branch, and I swung it in his direction with all my might.

What happened next was a confused blur. On my knees, I swung from left to right and back again in Jumbo's direction to keep him from getting a good fix on me. I whirled and spun until I felt sick to my stomach.

Then from behind me I heard a fearsome snarl, and something sailed past my shoulder. I had a hard time for a moment realizing that the dark-furred ferocity that had attached itself to Jumbo's thigh just above his left knee was Obie.

Jumbo screamed, an eerie, high-pitched sound that was clear and unarticulated terror. He struggled wildly, thrashing like I'd done the moment before, and Obie growled like a tiger.

Then I saw Jumbo lift his rifle over his head and smash it downward at Obie. I heard the thud and a sound like wood splintering, and I cried out, 'No! No-oo-ooo-o!'

Beyond the confused figures of Jumbo and the dog, outlined with a hard gold edge by the barn pole light, I saw Tunes, running back down the slope toward us.

Obie's jaws remained clamped, even after his body sagged. Jumbo tried to take a step, but Obie, all hundred pounds of him, dragged limply on Jumbo's leg, his teeth still embedded in the muscle above Jumbo's knee. Obie growled again, a fierce, gurgling snarl of a sound that struck an instant fear even in me. Then he was quiet.

Obie's clenched teeth let me know he was still alive. In the face of the blow he'd suffered, I was sure it was by sheer will. I fumbled to my feet. Jumbo had dropped his rifle as he struggled to pry open the dog's jaws. I attacked Jumbo, screaming wildly and beating on his bent back with my fists.

And then Tunes was there, grabbing up the gun and aiming it at Jumbo. For a moment I was scared she'd shoot, end the struggle right there and get even with Jumbo in one justifiable squeeze of the trigger.

'You best not move,' she said, looking straight down the barrel into Jumbo's eyes. Her voice was so calm it chilled me to the bone. 'You put your arms over your head,' she said to Jumbo. He hesitated a brief moment, then slowly raised his arms.

Obie still clung to Jumbo's leg.

'Obie, let go,' I said softly. Jumbo made soft groany noises in his throat. He stood there with his arms raised and shook his leg for all he was worth. 'Come, Obie,' I said softly.

I reached for my wounded dog with outstretched arms. He whined softly, and I felt the sticky wetness of his blood on my fingers. At that instant his jaws relaxed, and he fell against me with a sharp whine.

'Tunes, don't shoot,' I said softly. Jumbo moaned and sat on the ground, holding his leg. He looked up at Tunes and she just stood there with the gun aimed at his head, about eighteen inches away.

I grabbed Tunes by the arm, but she shook me off. Her eyes were focussed down the gun barrel at Jumbo's face.

'I'm going to see you go to jail,' she said through clenched teeth. She backed away, the gun still aimed at Jumbo.

I took Obie by his strong leather collar and half dragged, half pulled him along behind me. After a few seconds he organized his legs a bit better and stumbled after me in a crooked little trot.

Jumbo made apelike noises of pain and fear behind us, but I could see he was recovering his composure, and we barely had a second to get out of there.

Tunes looked over her shoulder, back at Jumbo, as if she wished she'd pulled the trigger.

'Come on,' I said. I took Obie's collar again, and with my other hand I grabbed Tunes and pulled her so hard I was afraid I'd detach her arm from her shoulder and take it along with me, leaving her behind.

'Don't be stupid!' I sounded foreign to myself, like someone far away had spoken.

Then Jumbo lurched toward us, still moaning and cursing like a madman, his legs beginning to coordinate under him.

'Move, Tunes,' I said. 'He'll kill us with his bare hands. Move!' The last 'Move!' was a terrified croak that shook her out of her trance. By then Obie was moving better, too. Tunes took a few hesitant steps in the direction I'd set, and the momentum of my running and hauling on her propelled her behind me, carrying Jumbo's .22. Then we were headed down the hill, our eyes able to see enough of the way in the predawn twilight to keep on our tree-dodging course back to the skiff.

I turned once and looked back, but Jumbo was not behind us, and I felt a brief thrill of victory.

We stumbled out into the creek to the tump that held the skiff. I helped Obie in and pushed us out into the water. Obie lay on his side on the floorboards, silent and motionless, and I didn't know whether he would make it. It was too shallow to start the engine, but I rowed quickly out to where it was deep enough, and the engine sang to life on the first pull.

Then Tunes took the stern seat to steer. I kept looking back, thinking how close we'd come – to being shot, to losing Obie, to losing everything.

Chapter 17

The skiff chattered swiftly over the choppy water of the protected creek. We made a long sliding arc out into the treacherous open water of the Bay, where the current and wind took up behind us, and headed straight for Judge's place.

I felt dizzy and disoriented, like my body really was somewhere else and I only imagined I was there with Tunes and Obie. The boat bucked forward as it cleared each crest, and glided down into each trough like a slow-motion roller coaster.

Tunes navigated by sheer instinct, steering over invisible shoals and sandbanks without a thought of them. Several times the engine screamed as it cleared the water. Obie laid his head on my foot. A pool of blood gathered beneath him.

I kept saying to myself, over and over, as if to pin myself down to the time and place, to make myself grasp what-all had happened, 'We're going to make it! We're going to make it!'

The sky was still roily with storm clouds, and the wind picked up the tops of waves, just where the water hung suspended, and hurled them against our soaked backs. The horizon glowed and the sky turned from grey to a faint yellow – it was getting on for five o'clock.

Tunes was grim-faced, and I knew her heart was filled with doubt. Although she trusted Judge, she was sure Sheriff would not see things our way. Looking down a gun barrel at Jumbo had gotten to her. Her sense of justice won out, and she was willing to take a terrible chance to bring him down. But she was not one bit comfortable with it.

I, on the other hand, was equally sure Sheriff would believe us. That everyone had acted bravely and we were safe seemed somehow to be in accord with our having done the right thing. And so it was inconceivable to me that Sheriff wouldn't see the truth for what it was. I was positive we had what Judge had called 'a case'.

We sped clear into Judge's creek. Our wake nudged the fishing boats still harder into the docks, their tethers strung taut on the storm tide like stabled horses spooked by the thunder and lightning. At Judge's landing the Bay washed over the dock and Tunes ran the skiff up on the shore.

The storm tide up here in the creek was much higher than normal. We stepped out onto Judge's lawn, three or four feet of which was underwater. I lifted Obie to his feet and out of the skiff. He moved slowly and gingerly.

I came slowly behind Tunes up through the garden to Judge's back door, pulling on Obie's collar and encouraging him every step of the way. Tunes hesitated for a moment. I smiled what I hoped was an encouraging smile, then knocked on the door.

Mrs Wickham came down in her bathrobe several minutes later, scowling through the panes of the back window.

We must have been a sorry sight, all three of us soaked through and looking scared as rabbits, Obie covered in blood. When she saw us, Mrs Wickham pursed her lips and her mouth worked, saying something we couldn't hear. She walked back through the kitchen as if she had no intention of letting us in.

'What if she's calling Sheriff?' Tunes said. She started to back up. I was afraid she'd bolt again, and I grabbed her by the arm.

'It's going to be okay,' I said. 'This is the right thing to do!'

At that second the kitchen lights came on and then the outside back lights. Judge's old basset hound, Thrum, waddled into the kitchen and bayed, swaying from side to side on her front feet. Obie growled softly. I tightened my grip on Tunes' arm and Obie's collar. Then Judge himself was at the door in a frayed flannel robe, his hair all standing up on end, his eyes squinting in the light.

'It's me and Tunes and Obie,' I shouted through the door.

His hands fumbled with the latch. Mrs Wickham stood behind him, scowling. Judge was always getting involved in other folks' business, and dragging it home with him, where far's she was concerned it wasn't welcome.

'Hold your horses,' Judge said, fumbling with the screen door, which also was locked. It seemed it would take him forever.

'Does your daddy know you're out?' Mrs Wickham asked, leaning past Judge to peer into my face just as soon as the door opened. 'I'm of a mind to call him.'

Then she looked at Tunes. And at Obie.

'What's this?' she asked, softening when she saw that sorry, bloody-headed dog. Evidently Mrs Wickham was more moved by animals than kids, for which I couldn't rightly blame her.

'Now, Claire,' Judge said. 'I've been waiting for Buck and Tunes. It's all right. You go on and get them something hot to drink and some towels. I'll call the vet and ask him to meet you at the clinic to see about this poor dog.'

She looked at him critically for a moment as if to evaluate how much sense he was making. She clucked her tongue and turned her back to us, then left the kitchen.

'You three are wetter'n last Sunday's newspaper,' Judge said, bending to examine the wound over Obie's eye. 'That looks nasty.' He seemed relieved to see us. 'Come on in and get dried off.'

Mrs Wickham strode back through the kitchen, a pile of towels stacked clear up under her chin.

'. . . catch your death,' she muttered and set them down on the table. 'Tunes, you go get your clothes off in the bathroom behind the kitchen. Buck, you come in here.' She shook out two terry bathrobes that were clean but raggedy and gave us each one. Then she set to rubbing Obie's fur dry. He licked her hand gratefully.

Tunes came back in her robe, which brushed low on the backs of her calves. Her eyes looked dazed, and she shivered.

Once we were dry, Mrs Wickham trundled off to get dressed while Judge called the veterinarian. Tunes and I went into the keeping room. Judge motioned us onto the couch, which faced the fireplace.

'So,' he said, laying the telephone receiver back in its cradle, 'the vet will be there when they arrive. Tell me what you have to tell. I'll make us a fire.'

Judge took away the needlepoint fire screen Mrs Wickham had placed in front of the fireplace for summer. She came in then dressed and wearing rain shoes, carrying some cotton flannel blankets. She looked with puckered disapproval at Judge about to mess up her clean hearth. Judge picked some fatwood sticks out of a kettle, reached into the woodbin, and laid a fire in the basket.

'I remembered after I left here that Kneebone's hound had his head bashed in, too, before he was shot,' I said when Judge finally sat.

Mrs Wickham reappeared with a tray of mugs filled with hot chocolate. She set it on the table. Then she whistled softly to Obie, who got up painfully.

'Go on, boy,' I said. 'It's all right.' He put his head down and dutifully followed Mrs Wickham through the door.

Tunes and I alternated sentences, telling every detail of what had happened from the time I arrived at the duck blind. Our voices were flat, almost mechanical, as if the night had sapped all of our energy. But we talked rapidly, taking care with our words to give the most complete picture, trying to get through it, correcting each other only to clarify a point or add an important detail.

Orange light from the fire flickered on Tunes' dark skin, which looked powdery in patches, dry from her living outdoors. Judge listened quietly, watching our faces intently.

'I was going to shoot Mr Rawlin,' Tunes said. 'I just couldn't pull the trigger. I kept thinking what you said, Buck, that killing's evil, and if I killed him it'd be just as evil as him killing Jorge. I was so afraid to come here, to go to Sheriff.'

Tunes crossed her arms at the elbows and bowed her head into their crook. Judge pulled her in against his side, tucking each of us under a shoulder, cradled like little children.

After a moment I said, 'I'm proud of you, Tunes, for not killing Jumbo.' My teeth chattered, and my voice had a hard time getting past the thick lump in the middle of my throat. 'This is all Jumbo's fault, not yours. You didn't do anything wrong!'

'Lord, Lord, what you two have been through,' said Judge, holding on to us both like he was afraid we'd fly away.

Eventually we sat back and dried our faces on the sleeves of our robes, while Judge made little clucking sounds over us. When we were steady enough, he handed each of us a mug of hot chocolate. We were quiet then except for pulling the chocolate in over our lips in small slurps.

'I know you've been through a lot,' Judge said to Tunes, 'but we need to talk about what you think Jumbo's motive might've been.'

I looked at Tunes. She leaned forward and set her mug on the table in front of her. So calm, so confident was Judge, Tunes didn't even hesitate.

'Yessir,' she said. And then, without a trace of emotion, she told every detail, starting with what Jumbo'd done to her since she was eleven years old. Her words made me wince almost like I was hearing them for the first time, only it was worse knowing already what had happened to her. I felt ill and shaken all over again.

Judge listened, looking away every once in a while. The fire burned lively and warm, cutting the post-storm chill and throwing little glints across Tunes' face, which was still as stone all the while she talked.

Toward the end of her telling of it, Judge stood and fished a handkerchief from the pocket of his robe. He paced the worn wooden floor, his old leather slippers shooshing back and forth. After she'd finished, he didn't speak for several minutes. Tunes just stared into the fire. Judge took one fierce, final swipe at each eye, blew his nose, and crammed the handkerchief back into his pocket.

'You two had better rest here a piece,' he said then, his voice all husky. 'You don't want Jumbo to come looking for you. I think it'd be best if I talk to Sheriff first. You'll be safe here.'

'H-h-how long will it take?' Tunes asked. Now her story was finished, it was like she couldn't keep her body under control. Her teeth chattered together wildly. As we sat there, swathed in blankets before the fire, shivering like it was midwinter, I was sure Judge's confidence had finally won her over.

'I don't rightly know,' said Judge. 'Not long, I'd say. But I should tell Sheriff what you've told me. We'd best get this cleared up right quick.'

He stood and reached across his desk for the telephone. I looked over at Tunes, whose eyes were fixed and starting. Ever so faintly her eyelids fluttered, like they were trying hard to stay open.

'Sheriff, Judge Wickham here,' said Judge, his voice firm with the old tone of authority for which everyone in Virginia's two Eastern Shore counties had respected him until not too long ago. 'I've got some important business I'd like to discuss with you . . .

'Yes, yes,' said Judge with some impatience. 'I wouldn't call you at this hour unless it was an emergency . . . I'd rather not say on the telephone. Okay, I'll meet you at your office in fifteen minutes.'

Judge stood and straightened his robe.

'You two had better get some sleep. I'll stop by and tell your folks you're here.'

I didn't feel like I could move, and was glad not to be going home.

He laid us down on opposite ends of the long leather couch and tucked pillows under our heads, the cotton flannel blankets around us. There, before the dying fire, now we had purged ourselves of the night's horrors, nothing was so irresistible as sleep.

The last thing I saw before I fell off the edge of consciousness was the pale watery sun coming through as it burned off the storm clouds outside the keeping room window, which faced out over the creek.

Chapter 18

I woke up drenched in sweat. The room was hot. The fire was dead on the hearth, the air acrid with its smell. The sun glared out on the water with a force like the inside of a furnace. All that was left of the storm was a white-hot mist.

For a moment I couldn't reckon where I was. I looked around the room and focused on Judge's maroon leather lawbooks lining the walls and his grey sweater draped over the back of a reading chair. And there was Tunes still asleep at the other end of the couch, one arm flung out, parallel to the floor, the other bent over her eyes.

A closing door must have awakened me, because within a few seconds Judge came in from the kitchen, Sheriff and Dad right behind him. I was totally unprepared for what happened next.

They were all quiet and purposeful, as if they had something important to do.

Sheriff strode across the room to the couch and stood over Tunes, who was still asleep. After a second he reached for the back pocket of his trousers. I didn't have a clue to what he was fixing to do until I saw the silver flash of the handcuffs.

He clicked one cuff around the wrist of her outstretched arm, reached over and took the arm crooked over her eyes, straightened it, and clicked the other cuff over that wrist.

'Wait!' I said. 'There's some mistake! Judge?'

I was fully awake then, and leaned up on my elbow, trying to get myself sitting. Tunes struggled toward consciousness.

Then all of a sudden her eyebrows shot up and her upper body lunged forward in a lightning-quick reflex, only to realize with perplexity her hands were shackled and she couldn't put them behind her to push herself up.

Dad crossed the room and knelt before me. Judge stood still, his eyebrows working, looking at the floor.

'We can explain!' I said, looking from Dad to Judge to Sheriff. 'You got to listen to Tunes! She didn't kill Jorge. Didn't you tell them, Judge? Why're you doing this?'

'I'm sorry, Buck,' was all Judge could say. His eyebrows worked, up and down, furrowing his brow, straightening it again. Sheriff's mouth was set in a hard line, and he said nothing.

Judge's transformation in just two hours from calm confidence to frail confusion inspired in me a terrible rage. Even as I exploded, I knew it was unjust to blame Judge. My anger was aimed at the way things were turning out, not at him, really.

'Sorry! Is that all you can say? You have a man who thinks nothing of killing and you're letting them blame an innocent person? Tunes's been hurt bad by Jumbo Rawlin. Didn't you tell them, Judge?' I demanded. Judge cleared his throat as if he would speak, but then he looked at the floor.

Dad had knelt down beside me where I struggled to get out of the nest of leather cushions. He slipped onto the seat beside me. He hadn't shaved, and the skin around the blue-black stubble on his chin was damp with sweat. His smell was warm and pungent, of coffee and sweat and line-dried shirt.

'Now, Buck,' he said, 'what looks like motive to you is information that has been turned around. Doesn't prove anything.'

'What do you mean?' I asked. 'Information from Tunes means less than information from Jumbo Rawlin?' Nobody spoke.

Sheriff waited for Tunes to wake up a bit more, and then he hauled on her wrists, trying to lift her to her feet. She came up by the handcuffs, her arms still bent. The bathrobe was twisted up around her hips, and her long brown legs thrashed to get under her. She struggled in an effort to pull down and straighten the robe, but she couldn't do anything with her hands tethered like that.

The robe pulled apart at the top, and she tried to get her hands loose from Sheriff to clutch it back together, but Sheriff hung on. We all averted our eyes from her faded cotton panties and the deep V of skin between her breasts. She made a little sound in her throat as she struggled, but she didn't protest. Seeing her forced into such indignity refuelled my fury.

'Stop it!' I shouted, my voice splintering like I was about to lose it. 'What's the matter with you?' I tried to disentangle myself from the blankets and my robe and Dad's arms to get up, but Dad held on to me.

Without acknowledging either of us, Sheriff began to recite in a low monotone: 'Tunes Smith, you are under arrest for the murder of Jorge Rodrigues. You have the right to remain silent. You have the right to counsel. Anything you say can and will be used against you . . .'

Tunes' eyes darted wildly from me to Sheriff to Judge, and back among our faces again, looking for a way out like a deer trapped in the headlights of a speeding truck.

'Do something! Dad! Judge!' That time I got myself free, but Dad reached out his long arm and caught me before I could cross to where Tunes stood, head straight forward and chin out, beside Sheriff.

None of them said a word, and I was ashamed of them all, grown men humiliating a proud girl like Tunes.

'You'll see,' I said, my voice an infuriatingly thin croak. I'd never been as angry before, nor have I since. 'Mr Rawlin shot Jorge. We can tell you his motive.'

'Buck, Miss Tunes'll have a chance to tell her story in court,' said Sheriff. 'We found her gun in Little Creek, near where you found the body. Ballistics tests show it was the gun killed Jorge Rodrigues. And you had no business hiding her. That's obstruction of justice.'

'You got everything turned back to front!' I shouted. 'Jumbo took Tunes' gun. Why do you take Mr Rawlin's word and not Tunes'?' I stared at Sheriff in disbelief.

'Mr Rawlin heard somebody outside his house last night,' Sheriff went on patiently. 'He went downstairs and found you two sneaking around his property. He said you set your dog on him, Buck, and then you both ran off with his gun. He came on up to the house to report these strange goings-on to me before first light this morning, before I ever heard from Judge. Now, a guilty man isn't likely to call the sheriff – '

'No!' I shouted. 'That's just it! He was counting on you believing him instead of Tunes. He was going to shoot Tunes and then he was going to shoot me, and Obie latched hold o' him. He'll have bite marks on his leg. He bashed Obie's head, just like Jorge's. And Kneebone's hound. He killed Jorge just like he killed the dog. And his motive – you'll see!'

'Buck, what you're telling me is nothing I don't already know.'

Sheriff had Tunes by the elbow now, and with her hands held tight together in the cuffs she rubbed her wrists against the bathrobe to get it straightened. She blinked her eyes rapidly, like she was trying not to cry.

'Tunes has worked right hard to construct a story so's you'd believe her, Buck, so's you'd help her. But I can show probable cause right now, plus assault, trespassing, plus refusing to cooperate . . . Your friend's under arrest, and you're in a peck of trouble, too.'

'You told me Tunes'd be all right!' I shouted at Judge. 'How could you be so . . . so . . .' I couldn't finish. I knew all too well it wasn't Judge's fault. 'I'm sorry,' I said, and then to add to my frustration and humiliation, I cried bitterly.

Tunes looked defiant now, watching us like she had nothing to do with any of us, like she thought we were crazy.

Dad stepped closer and hugged me to him. I struggled until he let me go.

'Tunes, say something!' I shouted.

'Why?' she asked. Her eyes and voice were calm and steely. 'You think anybody in this room's going to believe me? Buck Smith, I'd never trust you again, not if you were the last person on earth, not in a million years.'

Judge broke his silence then.

'Tunes does have a case,' he said. His voice was hoarse, and he looked as if he had no energy. 'Once Sheriff's heard what Tunes has to say . . . You two will have to be patient.'

Tunes made a defiant little gesture with her chin, and her breath came out in a 'Hmph!' My heart sank. How could I believe in Judge now – or any of them for that matter – when our hopes had been raised so high, only to come crashing down?

Just then Kneebone came into the kitchen and knocked on the doorframe. Sheriff waved him in. Kneebone walked in quietly, uneasily, and looked from face to face.

When he saw Tunes' hands were manacled, he went straight to her and put his arms around her. She couldn't hug him back, just stood there, her hands against her chest. He grabbed fistfuls of the terry robe that hung loosely over the sash at her waist and drew it tight around her, then pressed her fiercely against him again.

'What are you doing with my child?' Kneebone asked then, looking over her shoulder at Sheriff. His voice was very deep and soft.

'I'm taking her in, charging her with the murder of Jorge Rodrigues. Look here, Kneebone,' Sheriff said gruffly. 'You want to see your daughter, you follow us on down to the jail. I'll have to question her there.'

Kneebone lowered his head and buried his face into Tunes' shoulder. Tunes stood nearly as tall as Kneebone.

All she was able to do was tilt her head to the side and rest it against his bare brown skull, and let him hug her a moment before Sheriff led her away.

'You coming down to the jail?' Sheriff asked, turning to Kneebone and motioning us all toward the door. Kneebone put one big gnarled hand up over his face for a moment. He was unable to answer. He nodded his head. Sheriff turned to Dad and me.

'I want Buck down for questioning, too. You can bring him along in about an hour and a half, Senior, if you would. He's not a suspect right at this moment. But he's got some to answer for, helping Tunes and lying and all.' Dad nodded, his face all squeezed up into knots.

'For the love of the Lord,' Dad said in a tone of voice I'd never heard him use before, 'at least let them get dressed!'

Sheriff hesitated, then said to Tunes, 'Go on, get dressed if you like. You got two minutes.' He unlocked the handcuffs and motioned her toward the bathroom.

Tunes' eyes glinted fierce and falcony, and I could see she'd pulled that old familiar shield about her so nobody on earth could touch her.

I sensed then with a sickening realization Tunes was right. Nobody would believe her, and she would be blamed after all. I felt all panicky inside. I'd been so sure I was right! How had Judge failed us so badly?

165

They left a few minutes later, and Judge and Dad and I stood looking at each other. Judge cleared his throat.

'I'm sorry, Buck,' he said again, softly. I just nodded my head.

I hated myself for thinking it, but what Dad had said about Judge dropping his sails echoed through my mind. At that moment Judge looked very tired and sick.

Chapter 19

Dad took me home before we went down to Sheriff's office. He was silent the entire way. Mama ran out and hugged me to her.

'Obie's going to be fine, son,' she said, hugging me and hugging me, near the point of suffocation. 'The vet wants to keep him for a few days to watch him.' I was relieved at least at that.

Gran insisted on feeding us scrambled eggs. Far back as I could remember, wasn't a major event went by without the table being loaded with stacks of toast, big breakfast plates, a bowl of eggs, grits, bacon, juice and coffee. She even did it the morning after Granddaddy died.

When we were all seated around the table with plates in front of us, I told them the whole story. When I'd finished, nobody moved for a full minute.

The house seemed empty without Obie, and I thought of how close I'd come to losing him. Mama and Dad and Gran were silent. The whole house was silent, so that the screech of an osprey flying over the garden carrying a fish home to her babies made us all start.

Dad looked like something was chewing on him terrible. Far's I was concerned, there wasn't anything further to say. After a bit Dad got up slowly from his chair and came around to where I sat. He took my face between his hands and looked into my eyes. He pulled me up and clasped me against him and held me there hard.

'I was so afraid for you, son,' Dad said, holding on to me for dear life. 'Afraid of Tunes' influence on you, afraid she'd

167

done wrong and would take you along down her difficult road. I still don't know. The evidence Sheriff has could go either way. I'm not sure what I believe, but I did have an obligation to Tunes and Kneebone and I didn't meet it. I don't know if they'll accept my help now, but I have to try.'

When he let go, I looked up and Gran was wiping tears from her eyes.

'Seems the price of loyalty's mighty dear around here,' Gran said dryly. She tucked her handkerchief into her apron and set to clearing the still mostly full dishes from the table.

Mama sat unravelling the edge of her place mat. It was always difficult to know what she was thinking. Still is, and I'm five years older now. Sometimes Mama seems lost in her own world, which revolves around the garden club, bridge, the farm, the house. She loves us, but sometimes it seems she doesn't quite rise to the occasion.

'Sheriff is bound and determined Tunes is guilty,' I said. 'Do you think he'll believe her once he's heard from her own mouth what Jumbo's done to her?'

'I don't know, Buck,' Dad said. 'I believe Sheriff'll act according to how he sees the evidence. One thing sure, Tunes's going to need a good lawyer. I know you love Judge, but you can see it isn't fair to put that kind of responsibility on him. He can help us find somebody good. We can raise the money to pay for a lawyer somehow. Lord knows Kneebone can't afford a lawyer's fees.'

'However are we going to afford a lawyer?' Mama asked. I thought of Dad telling me how sometimes it was difficult to face the truth when it rearranged what-all you thought about the world, and I tried not to be angry with Mama.

'We'll manage somehow,' Dad said.

We stayed near about two hours in the waiting room at

the front of the building that held Sheriff's office and the jail until we were called in for questioning.

The public defender passed us on his way out. It was a hot day and he wore a heavy wool tweed jacket. I wondered how much sense he had. Dad was right about Tunes needing a good lawyer.

I sat with my spine pressed flat against the straight-backed wooden bench. Tunes had been taken over to detention in Norfolk by the time I went in and faced Sheriff across his broad desk.

For the third time that morning I told the story of what'd happened, from the time I saw Jumbo out poking around in the creek with his boathook, through finding the body, and Tunes telling me what Jumbo'd done to her, Jumbo bashing in Obie's head, then going to Judge.

By then the telling was difficult. I was drained and exhausted. I had to search for words, and once I found them they came out in a flat monotone without feeling or emphasis. Looking back on it, I wondered if Sheriff might have not credited the full truth of what I said because there was no emotion left in me.

'Well,' said Sheriff when I'd done, 'at least your story matches Tunes'.' He questioned me on a few points, but when that was done he had nothing more to say.

Late that afternoon Dad and I walked over to Kneebone's to tell him we would help find a lawyer and the money to pay for it.

Things had happened so fast I hardly had time to take stock. But I felt at least like my father was back on my side as we walked together down the dirt track to Kneebone's. It felt like one part of my life had been reconstructed. Up until then I'd begun to feel everything had changed and nothing good had taken the place of what-all had gone. Maybe Dad couldn't bring himself to believe Tunes completely yet, but at least he was standing behind me and wanted to help her. It made me hope he'd come to believe her sooner or later.

Mazie and Jep were there, sitting on Kneebone's stoop. Mazie came and hugged me. Jep just sat.

'Where's Kneebone?' Dad asked. Jep tilted his head toward one shoulder, through the front door toward the living room. Dad didn't hold too much with Jep.

Kneebone sat on the edge of the seat of his rocking chair, his elbows on his knees, head bowed, holding one gnarled hand in the other and staring at them. I knew when I saw him like that he knew what Jumbo'd done to Tunes, and how Jorge'd died.

The light inside the house was dim. The sun was near setting across the Bay, and the shadows of trees fell across the windows.

Kneebone looked up when we came in. Jep and Mazie stayed out on the stoop.

'I been a fool, Kneebone,' Dad began. 'I want Tunes to have the best lawyer we can find. We'll find a way – '

'We already got a lawyer and money to pay for it,' Jep said through the screen door. He'd stood on the top step of the stoop and turned around to listen. 'We don't need your help.'

The Reverend King Saloman Jones called meetings in all of the black churches and talked to folks about what'd happened. They took up a collection for Tunes' defence. Dad sent a cheque, and the Reverend came to thank him for his contribution.

I don't know how much Dad gave, but it must've been a lot.

Mama stood in the kitchen discussing it with him one morning. She wrung her hands, then brought them up to her mouth and chewed on one knuckle. When Dad had finished what he was saying, she didn't reply for a long time, and for several days after she didn't smile when she talked to him. She didn't smile at all, come to think of it.

I was sitting on Granddaddy's old chair on the dock one evening after supper about a week after Tunes' arrest, watching the fireflies up toward the rose garden.

A car pulled into the driveway, crunching over the oystershells, its headlights bobbing golden-yellow down the lane behind the house. After a bit I headed on up, putting Granddaddy's chair away in the shed as I came.

Outside the kitchen door Dad stood with the Reverend, who wore the same seersucker suit, black shirt and clerical collar and a straw hat. Dad just stood listening with his hands on his hips. In the twilight he looked uncomfortable, shifting his weight from foot to foot.

He motioned me over to them and laid his arm across my shoulders. It was just after sunset, and darkness was coming on.

'Son, this is the Reverend King Salomon Jones . . .'

'Yessir,' I said. 'I know.' This time the Reverend held his large hand out to me. I hesitated only a moment before I shook it.

His brow was gathered in a larger-than-life frown, and the rest of his broad face hung down in creases.

'Buck, I hear tell you've done everything in your power to help Tunes.' I shrugged. For the first time in several days I felt my throat tighten and tears at the back of my eyes.

'I just came to thank you for trying to help her, and to thank your daddy for his generous contribution to Tunes' defence fund.' His voice, when he had a mind to be kindly, was deep and melodious. 'Now she needs your prayers.'

The lawyer they hired was an African American from Richmond named Redman Allworth. His picture in the paper showed a tall, slender man with close-cropped greying hair, a long face and serious eyes. It said he'd been involved in civil rights cases all over the state, and he'd even been up to Washington to testify before Congress.

For all folks were impressed with Mr Allworth, there was talk that Kneebone should have hired a local lawyer who knew Tunes and knew the Eastern Shore, but I guess with all that money collected by the Reverend King Saloman Jones, he felt it was somewhat out of his hands.

I don't know much about the trial. Juvenile Court sits behind closed doors. When the state's attorney called on me to testify, Tunes watched as I walked to the witness box beside the judge, directly across from Mr Allworth. She wore a new flowered dress that looked like something Mama would've picked for her. When I looked at her she lowered her eyes slowly, and she never looked at my face again while I answered the state's attorney's questions.

He asked me to tell my side of the story, which I tried to do. He kept interrupting to discredit what-all I said. I had to admit I'd lied to Sheriff on several occasions. He never gave me a chance to explain, and he didn't ask a single thing that I could have answered in a way that would have helped Tunes.

When it was time for Mr Allworth to ask me questions he acted like he'd breathe easier the sooner I got down from my seat. So a lot of important facts that only I could tell never came out in the trial, such as how Jorge's head was stove in just like Kneebone's dog's.

When I did get down I looked again at Tunes. She sat up straight, chin out, her hands folded on the table before her. Her eyes stared off in that familiar falcony stare, and that's how I always remember her.

The rest Dad learned from Kneebone. The Reverend King Saloman Jones also testified on Tunes' behalf. I knew he meant well, but he didn't know Tunes at all, and he couldn't say much that was of help. The state's attorney got him to admit Tunes didn't ever go to church, and in fact that when she was little, she caused some trouble in Sunday school.

Well, anybody knew Tunes knew she hated Sunday school. She always said, 'If there's any way to better praise the Lord than going out in nature to worship Him, I don't know about it.' And she'd go fishing.

As it happened, Sheriff'd arrested Tunes on the sheer weight of Jumbo's word. When Tunes' gun was found, that was enough to make up his mind to come down on the side of Jumbo's version of things.

Jumbo denied ever assaulting Tunes. The state's attorney gave him the opportunity to tell about her 'romance' with Jorge. He also produced Mr Menendez and two other people whose stories agreed with Jumbo's. And that was that Tunes and Jorge had been lovers since that January.

Several witnesses also said they'd seen her trudging through the fields towards home very early some mornings wearing the same clothes she'd been seen in the day before. Kneebone and I knew she did that sometimes, spent the night somewheres out on the creek – in the duck blind, one time in the old oak tree over by the Timmons farm – but nobody got the chance to explain that to the judge.

Many was the time Mama clucked her tongue when Kneebone stopped by looking for Tunes. Mama'd come up to make sure I was tucked in some summer nights, just to be sure I wasn't out with her.

What it came down to was Tunes' word against Jumbo's. And despite folks being afraid of him – or maybe because of it – he carried a lot of respect in the community. And everything Tunes and I said in her defence was discredited.

In the end *The Eastern Shore News* reported there was not enough evidence to convict Tunes of manslaughter in the death of Jorge Rodrigues. Her attorney asked the judge to drop the charges for insufficient evidence. The judge made it clear he did so reluctantly.

From that time on, Jumbo took a lower profile in the community. It added even more to his reputation for being peculiar. But near as I could tell, he just went on like he always had done.

The Reverend King Saloman Jones and Mr Redman Allworth proclaimed the state's failure to convict Tunes a great victory for justice. But most folks on the Eastern Shore didn't regard it as such. Some were mad she wasn't convicted. Others felt bad her name hadn't been cleared despite her not being convicted. All it meant was she didn't have to go to jail. Knowing Tunes, if she had a choice she'd rather have a clear name.

Judge died just a couple of months later. Had a stroke and never regained consciousness. I believe he died as a result of his disappointment at what had happened to Tunes, a broken heart, you might say. It still seems to me Judge had been right about what we needed to do. Because of his spells it seemed Sheriff didn't credit him with any competence whatever.

And Kneebone's health began to fail, so he was forced to leave a lot to Jep.

Dad never was able to believe in Tunes' innocence. He never said as much, but I could tell by the way he tugged at his chin whenever anybody talked about the evidence of the case. Dad was a rigid man for whom there were no shades of meaning when it came to good and bad. But he'd decided that loyalty counted for a lot with family, and he'd remembered almost in time that Tunes was family. Almost but not quite.

As for me, it never once occurred to me to doubt her. I never heard Tunes Smith utter a false word. There were plenty of times she was wrong, but she always told things exactly as she saw them, taking the consequences as they came.

After the trial was over, I rushed over to Kneebone's to see Tunes. She'd been in detention for nearly three months, and I just wanted to lay eyes on her and tell her how happy I was to have her back.

I guess I expected she'd come back to school in the fall and we'd still be friends. I knew it wouldn't be like before, but I didn't have any thought of changing our friendship more than we had to because of what-all had happened.

I skidded my bicycle around the edge of Kneebone's yard, only to find the place all shut up, the curtains hanging in that empty-house way, the red geraniums in pots on the stoop by the front door drooping from neglect. I went back later that day, and then again still later, and the next day and the next.

Finally, a week later, Kneebone showed up, looking years older than when I'd last seen him during the trial. His face was haggard and grey, and his shoulders hung like the geraniums in the pots.

'She's gone for good this time, Buck, sure,' he said, nodding slowly. 'I have to trust in the Lord to keep her safe.'

'She didn't leave a message for me?' I couldn't keep the incredulity from my voice.

Kneebone shook his head back and forth once, then reached out for me. He pressed his gnarled elbows into my back, then held me at arm's length to look into my face.

'She loved you more than anybody, Buck,' he said softly. 'But the good old times are gone forever. Now you go on home and get on with your life. Even if she did come back, it wouldn't be the same.'

But I knew that much already. I'd tried my darndest to pull back to the way things'd been between us. But the wounds were beyond healing. Time could not be replayed, and the only thing left was to go on with our lives the best we could, like Kneebone said.

I started out by writing her every day, all that was happening on the farm, in the woods, and on the water – when the owls were after the baby rabbits, when the otter pups learned to swim – all the things she and I'd occupied ourselves with, and that I knew she'd want to hear. I gave the letters to Kneebone to mail for me.

Tunes wrote Kneebone a few times to see how he was and say she was fine. But she made him promise he wouldn't tell anybody where she was. I guess she figured we all were better off without her. I hated it that she underestimated my friendship, even associated me with the betrayal.

Kneebone did tell me she was with relatives, people who cared for her. I knew she had her mama's folks down in Carolina, but Kneebone and Mazie also had relatives over in Norfolk. It was a big family.

When Obie came back, some of the light had gone out of him. He stayed beside me faithfully, never left me all the while I dug in the garden, ran the tractor, sat looking out over the creek. It seemed he had no heart for the Bay any more. When I went back to school, he'd go to the soybean field with me, and sometimes lie there all day long waiting for the school bus to come back.

After the first couple of months I cut back to writing Tunes just once a week, but I wrote faithfully. I missed her terribly then. I all but quit fishing, didn't take the skiff out for weeks on end.

In that time I had to keep reminding myself that this was Tunes' tragedy. It was her life was ruined, not mine.

And yet I couldn't help feeling sorry for myself. I'd lost Tunes, my best friend, and with her the notion that the world was basically a good place where if you did good, things'd turn out all right.

I'd also lost the notion there was magic in the world. I guess you could say I'd lost my childhood.

Sometimes I feared the worst for Tunes, and had visions of her being lost to the dangers of big-city streets. That was the worst Shore folks could imagine for kids.

But then I'd think how resourceful she'd been, taking care of herself in the duck blind, living off wild fennel and fish she'd caught with her bare hands, and I'd feel somewhat better.

Later I wrote less frequently, and finally I decided she didn't want to hear from me, so I stopped writing her altogether.

She came back several times to see Kneebone. He always told me afterward. She'd appear with no warning, stay a day and a night, then return to wherever she'd come from.

Kneebone hasn't been doing at all well this last winter. We were afraid he wasn't going to make it through to spring. Someone sent word to Tunes. She came one night and spent the night with him, then disappeared the next day.

She was still the light in his life, and he took solace in the fact she got away and was living a decent life where nobody knew what'd happened to her here.

Mama and Gran cooked a meal for Kneebone every night, and I took it over to him. His hands were so bad in the cold weather I had to build him a fire in the kitchen stove and then feed him in front of it before tucking him into his bed.

I guess if Tunes did come back to stay, she'd have pretty much a full-time job taking care of him. I don't know what'll happen to him. He can't work, but he has Social

Security. Mazie also comes by once a day to bring food and to see Kneebone's okay.

I used to try to talk to Kneebone about what happened. But his eyes would just fill up and he'd wave me away. So he and I talked mostly about the weather and the crops, which remained his chief interest even though he wasn't able to help Dad much on the farm any more.

Gran's the one I talk most to. But there's nothing that talking'll bring back, so we don't talk about what happened. In some respects we all went on as if that mysterious, gimlet-eyed girl who'd been such an important part of us never had existed at all.

Obie is old now and arthritic. We have a new dog named Warren, who's not nearly as good as Obie was at finding fish. But Warren's still young, not yet two. Once he's settled down, maybe he'll get serious about something important. Right now he jumps overboard every time a crab swims past.

As for me, after Tunes left, there was nothing here on the Shore for me. Because she'd shown me the magic the creatures brought to the mud and water and trees, being among them without her made me sad and guilty. Then slowly I began to see that all of nature worked in cycles, by some turns beautiful and miraculous, by others senseless and destructive. I learned to forgive, and I decided to stay on the Shore, on the farm. I just couldn't imagine living anywheres else.

I graduated high school this spring, and I'm going off to Virginia Polytechnic, where I'll study agriculture. I want to come back and work with Dad, take over the farm some day.

Last year, in our senior year of high school, Mabe Tucker and Brooks Dowd finally broke up, and Mabe and I have gone together ever since. She's going to Mary Baldwin College come September, and we've talked about getting married once we both have our degrees.

I still think about Tunes and me and the times we spent together on the Bay. They are the most important thing about my life.

This morning I was out poking around in the skiff looking for some trout to catch, and old Doke Watkins came puttering along in the *Dora Mae*. I waved.

'Ye catchin' anything, Buck?' he asked.

'No, sir, not yet,' I said.

''Bout th'only thing out there's bluefish. They're running thicker'n eelgrass,' he said. He turned to his bait barrels for a second, then back to me.

'Hear yer goin' to the Polytechnic in a few weeks,' he said. 'Got a scholarship!'

'Yessir,' I said.

'Well, congratulations, and don't you stay away from the Shore, hear?'

I smiled and waved, and he turned the *Dora Mae* out to check his crab pots.

I faced out toward deep water, and sure enough, the surface all around me rippled, and I could see for half a mile a school of menhaden flashing silver here and there, chased by a voracious tide of bluefish. Those blues come on like an army. Last spring they chased millions of menhaden up into the cordgrass along mile after mile of coast, setting all of Northampton County to stinking and buzzing with bluebottle flies like Chaney's north field the week after a fish fry.

The fuse was burning now, yellow flame climbing hungrily towards the bottle neck. He drew back his arm and threw without aiming. The bottle arced through the air trailing sparks . . .

When two young children are the victims of a racial attack, it leads friends Steve and Ashraf to question their friendship and loyalties. As their anger at events develops they find themselves getting drawn into a world of hatred and violence that threatens to destroy not only their friendship but the lives of those around them . . .

Age 12+   ISBN: 0 435 12501 X

Heinemann
New Windmills

Founding Editors: Anne and Ian Serraillier

Chinua Achebe Things Fall Apart
Vivien Alcock The Cuckoo Sister; The Monster Garden;
The Trial of Anna Cotman; A Kind of Thief; Ghostly Companions
Margaret Atwood The Handmaid's Tale
Jane Austen Pride and Prejudice
J G Ballard Empire of the Sun
Nina Bawden The Witch's Daughter; A Handful of Thieves; Carrie's
War; The Robbers; Devil by the Sea; Kept in the Dark; The Finding;
Keeping Henry; Humbug; The Outside Child
Valerie Bierman No More School
Melvin Burgess An Angel for May
Ray Bradbury The Golden Apples of the Sun; The Illustrated Man
Betsy Byars The Midnight Fox; Goodbye, Chicken Little; The
Pinballs; The Not-Just-Anybody Family; The Eighteenth Emergency
Victor Canning The Runaways; Flight of the Grey Goose
Ann Coburn Welcome to the Real World
Hannah Cole Bring in the Spring
Jane Leslie Conly Racso and the Rats of NIMH
Robert Cormier We All Fall Down; Tunes for Bears to Dance to
Roald Dahl Danny, The Champion of the World; The Wonderful
Story of Henry Sugar; George's Marvellous Medicine; The BFG;
The Witches; Boy; Going Solo; Matilda
Anita Desai The Village by the Sea
Charles Dickens A Christmas Carol; Great Expectations;
Hard Times; Oliver Twist; A Charles Dickens Selection
Peter Dickinson Merlin Dreams
Berlie Doherty Granny was a Buffer Girl; Street Child
Roddy Doyle Paddy Clarke Ha Ha Ha
Gerald Durrell My Family and Other Animals
Anne Fine The Granny Project
Anne Frank The Diary of Anne Frank
Leon Garfield Six Apprentices; Six Shakespeare Stories;
Six More Shakespeare Stories
Jamila Gavin The Wheel of Surya
Adele Geras Snapshots of Paradise

Alan Gibbons Chicken
Graham Greene The Third Man and The Fallen Idol; Brighton Rock
Thomas Hardy The Withered Arm and Other Wessex Tales
L P Hartley The Go-Between
Ernest Hemmingway The Old Man and the Sea; A Farewell to Arms
Nigel Hinton Getting Free; Buddy; Buddy's Song
Anne Holm I Am David
Janni Howker Badger on the Barge; Isaac Campion; Martin Farrell
Jennifer Johnston Shadows on Our Skin
Toeckey Jones Go Well, Stay Well
Geraldine Kaye Comfort Herself; A Breath of Fresh Air
Clive King Me and My Million
Dick King-Smith The Sheep-Pig
Daniel Keyes Flowers for Algernon
Elizabeth Laird Red Sky in the Morning; Kiss the Dust
D H Lawrence The Fox and The Virgin and the Gypsy;
Selected Tales
Harper Lee To Kill a Mockingbird
Ursula Le Guin A Wizard of Earthsea
Julius Lester Basketball Game
C Day Lewis The Otterbury Incident
David Line Run for Your Life
Joan Lingard Across the Barricades; Into Exile; The Clearance;
The File on Fraulein Berg
Robin Lister The Odyssey
Penelope Lively The Ghost of Thomas Kempe
Jack London The Call of the Wild; White Fang
Bernard Mac Laverty Cal; The Best of Bernard Mac Laverty
Margaret Mahy The Haunting
Jan Mark Do You Read Me? (Eight Short Stories)
James Vance Marshall Walkabout
W Somerset Maugham The Kite and Other Stories
Ian McEwan The Daydreamer; A Child in Time
Pat Moon The Spying Game
Michael Morpurgo Waiting for Anya; My Friend Walter;
The War of Jenkins' Ear
Bill Naughton The Goalkeeper's Revenge
New Windmill A Charles Dickens Selection
New Windmill Book of Classic Short Stories
New Windmill Book of Nineteenth Century Short Stories

How many have you read?

Josh groped his way out of sleep, immediately remembering that the twins had a secret.

Josh knows his brothers are hiding something from him – something so big and terrible that it is making Tom remote and Jack violent.

Struggling to understand what it is that is changing them . . . making them wicked . . . Josh is determined to get to the bottom of their secret. But is he prepared for the terrible truth of what they have done?

Age 13+   ISBN: 0 435 12505 2